Chronicles of the Fire Child

Written by Tessa Jensen
Illustrated by Lizzy D. Hill

To request permission, contact the publisher at
tessa-jensen@tessa-jensen.com

Paperback ISBN: 979-8-9858326-8-6
eBook ISBN: 979-8-9858326-9-3
Hardback: 979-8-9936370-0-6

First paperback edition November 2025

Cover art and illustrations by Lizzy D. Hill

Dedicated to the brave and curious children who change the world, and the mothers who lead them.

Table of Contents

Chronicle the First

Hiya Everyone! I'm Nova Jane Flaherty, and I'm seven years old. Some people call me the Fire Child because I have fire on my head and fire in my heart. This means I have bright red hair and I care with every little teeny tiny cell in my body. Most of the time, the fire in my heart helps keep me and the people I love warm. But, on occasion, I get flaming mad and say or do things I should not. Fire is a difficult natural element to control because it is both necessary and destructive.

I've noticed that a lot of adults have ashes in their hearts because somewhere along the way, someone extinguished their flames. I will not let that happen to me, I can tell you that for free!

Questions flame heart fires, that's why I ask so many. Did you know you can learn anything if you ask lots of questions? You can! I live in Doily Dayle with my great uncle, Mr. Pip. He's old and wears lederhosen and combs his bushy white mustache with a tiny toy comb meant for plastic ponies. He forgets his hearing aids most of the time, likes soup even on hot days, and toodles around the yard. I think he likes to bury his treasures because I saw him dig up and rebury a box recently. He put a big, concrete bird bath on top of it, so I think he would prefer I leave his treasure alone.

I think he's a little odd, which is good because I am also a little odd. I used to live far away in the Pacific Northwest with my family, but my mom and dad got sick and never woke up. So, now I have a new family, patchwork style.

Patchwork families are like patchwork quilts; you pick up the pieces that make you smile, and you sew them to the other pieces that make you smile until your collection is so big that it covers your heart. No more cold toes, no more cold tears. That's how it works.

I will tell you about my patches and why they make me smile.

Mr. Pip is my flannel patch because he is like a cozy grandpa who is always happy to see me.

Astrid is my flower patch. I know you know Astrid Beeswax because she is famous for her flower shop. She has black hair, green eyes, and wears fancy dresses every day of her life! She likes flowers, treats, promptness, and orderliness, which means she likes things to be where they are supposed to be, and not to be where they are not supposed to be. She's kind and generous, and sometimes I can see her swallow a mean word that's trying to escape off the tip of her tongue. Sometimes I think she might choke!

Her flower shop is called The Bee's Knees, and I go there almost every day of my life, basically. She is also next door neighbors with Mr. Pip, which means she is also my next door neighbor, which means she sees me frequently because the great out of doors is one of my usual haunts. Frequently means many times, and haunts, when used as a noun, means a place frequented by a person. A noun is a person, place, or thing. That's what Astrid taught me.

Roland is my strong patch. Roland is Astrid's twin brother, and he is married to Lottie Da. He is gentle, funny, and is a good taker carer. He is the head hockey coach at Doily Dayle's Moose University, and he likes to win. He says he hopes that every team they play has the best game of their lives, but the Moose still beats them. He says cheering for someone to have a bad game is bad form. Bad form means rude.

Beatrice is my nurture patch. She helps people grow! Beatrice is Astrid and Roland's mother, and Astrid lives with her. She is blind, but I didn't know until Mr. Pip told me. When she could see, she was a children's book illustrator. Astrid is lucky because her mom is in the kitchen waiting for her, no matter what time she comes home.

Jasper is my chicken patch. He is my real swell friend who likes to pretend to be a chicken and does not like having long hair. He only wants his mom to shave his blonde hair into a buzz cut. Jasper loves to see birds fly, and his eyes get teary when I cry.

Oswald is my broken clock patch. He is always in a hurry, constantly misplacing things, and never on time. He is the same ancientness as Mr. Pip, and still makes tiny toys for his shop, Oswald's Tiny Toys. He blinks a lot and loves to wear the same Kelly green cable knit sweater every day, the one with big wooden buttons. I asked him if he washed his sweater every night to keep it clean, and he said he has thirteen of the exact same one!

One time, while I was at The Bee's Knees, Oswald came in and asked me why I looked sad. I told him that a kid at school said that I was odd because I like to examine every classroom from each corner, so I can plan for possible koala bear attacks, since I recently learned that koala bears are not friendly. We, the people of this earth, have been making koala bear stuffies for a bajillion years, and they might get ticked if they learn we've been misrepresenting them and causing humans to invade their privacy in the wilds of the Australian outback.

Oswald said, "I don't know why people say 'odd' like it's a disease that can be avoided if you wash your hands. What's wrong with being unique?"

Do you know what unique means? Unique means unlike anything else. Mr. Pip told me this world doesn't have another Nova Jane Flaherty, so why should I try to be anyone but me?

I am unique in a super duper a million times of ways! For example, I remember what people say and how they say it, word for word.

Did you know that when people lie, their eyes and smiles don't match? Astrid noticed my talent when I pretended to be Thistlewhistle the parrot in her window at 6:03 am on a Saturday. Thistlewhistle belongs to Drimwella Spindlewitt, who owns the local craft store, Not Your Grandma's Doily Yarn and Lace.

Just like Thistlewhistle, I was repeating one of Astrid's funny conversations with Mr. Pip when she woke up and had a Scream Attack. I was wearing a beak I made from a glittery party hat and a shirt covered in red and blue feathers and sequins that I glued on myself!

She talked to Mr. Pip that afternoon, and they decided I needed to use my talent for something other than pretending to be a parrot and terrifying the delicious slumber of the unsuspecting and weary travelers of the world. So, Astrid designed a special reading and writing class for me on Tuesdays and Thursdays because she thinks I can change the world with my imagination. The entire world!

Reading and writing open doors. I thought my hands opened the doors, and when I tried to open my bedroom door with a book, it took forever. Astrid said I will learn what doors reading and writing can open as soon as I step through them. English is so confusing sometimes!

***

I like learning from Astrid because she listens to me, unlike my teacher at school, Crissy Hypo. No one likes it when people don't listen to them or tell them what to think, even kids! Adults don't remember how hard it is to be a kid with someone bossing you as soon as you wake up.

Jasper, my real swell friend, has a mom who yells, and yells, and yells! One time, when we were playing Sleep Attack in my backyard, she said, "I wish Jasper would sleep like that at night." And I told her he would probably sleep better if she did not yell so much. She got super duper a million times mad and made

Jasper go home. Jasper hung his head and wiped a tear from his eye.

My teacher is mean to Jasper, too. I can see her trying to stop smiling when she says something that makes him hang his head. Why do adults like to make kids hang their heads?

Jasper loves making bird noises because he loves birds, and he likes to share what he learns from his bird books. Every art project he makes turns into a cardinal or a peregrine falcon. He wants to be a falconer when he grows up, which means he wants to train falcons.

One day, before class started, I overheard at least three teachers talking about how stressed they were because the kids in their classes were annoying. They were in the hall, and I was putting away my coat and backpack. Miss Hypo said, "I don't like children but tolerate them. One mustn't leave the future to chance."

Don't you think that sounds a little rude? I did. I did not hear the rest of what they said because Jude the Dude asked me if I lost my art project in my hair. I told him my hair was my art project, and he said I would never win an art contest. So, I balled up my fists and screamed, and he started fake crying. Fake crying never solves anything and ruins soccer games. That's what Roland told me. He also told me that screaming never solves anything. But it stops me from throwing and kicking things.

My volume made Miss Hypo come running around the corner, see Jude the Dude's tears, and say, "Nova, I know you said something mean to Jude, or he wouldn't be crying like this. Look what you've done! You have hurt his feelings. If you make someone cry because you said something rude, you're supposed to say sorry. You should say sorry."

"I did not say anything rude. How do you know he is not fake crying?" I asked. She was wrong, so I wanted to know how she knew something that couldn't be known.

"Because, Nova, your scream would make anyone cry."

"But you said that you know I said something mean to Jude the Dude, or he wouldn't be crying like this, and now you are saying that he's crying because of my scream. So, you don't know what made him cry in the first place."

"I did not say any of those things. You misunderstood," Miss Hypo said with a big smile and angry eyes.

"Yes, you did, and no, I did not," I whispered.

Miss Hypo turned away from Jude the Dude, put her face way too close to mine, and said with peanut butter breath, "Excuse me, young lady. What makes you think you can talk to me like that? Apologize to Jude this instant!"

Jude the Dude started crying even louder while slowly squeezing tears out of his eyes.

"Well? Nova? Are you going to apologize to Jude for hurting his feelings? Where is your compassion?"

I looked straight into her angry eyes and said, "No."

The bell rang, and it was time for class to start, so she looked over her shoulder before saying, "Go sit down, and don't let me see or hear from you for the rest of the day."

Jude the Dude wiped his nose on his sleeve and winked at me as we walked to our seats. Being mean for fun is what makes someone a real bully.

As soon as Miss Hypo was done taking attendance, she began one of her lectures, "This morning, I was made aware of an unsettling situation in which one of our own students was unkind to another student. You, young as you are, are citizens of Doily Dayle and, as such, are expected to show respect and compassion to others. The list of rules I am about to read to you is not officially in print, but if all goes well, it soon will be. Listen closely. Do not make fun of others. Do not scream. Do not chew with your mouth open or within ten feet of me if possible; I really do hate mouth noises. Do not ask irrelevant questions. Do not use your imagination unless told to do so, and only imagine things from the list provided to you. Think as you are told to think, like what you are told to like, and you can easily fit in."

I raised my hand with some other kids, but she ignored us.

"Take out your worksheets. If you finish, I have more," she instructed. We did worksheets for at least a million hours. Then the bell rang.

First recess was sunny and happy! Jasper and I saw a blue jay and northern cardinals, and he got excited and told me everything he knew about the birds, which is basically everything there is to know. Did you know that the blue jay's feathers only look blue because their microscopic structure scatters light? What if my microscopic structure scattered glitter and sunshine? What would your microscopic structure scatter? Astrid's would scatter flowers.

When we walked back into our classroom, Jasper was chirping like a blue jay, and Miss Hypo got a mean look in her eye. "Jasper! I have told you over and over again to stop chirping like a bird. Every time you chirp, a real blue jay dies. Do you want to be responsible for their deaths?"

Jasper hung his head and wiped a tear from his eye again. What if he gets stuck like that? His shoulders started shaking, and Miss Hypo just watched him and said nothing. I wouldn't let my friend sit there and cry, so I walked over to hug him.

Miss Hypo raced me to his desk, stood between me and Jasper, and said, "Sit down now."

"Please, Miss Hypo. Be nice to Jasper. You told us this morning to show respect and compassion to others. Hugging someone who is crying is compassion. Plus, you were rude. If you make someone cry because you said something rude, you're supposed to say sorry. You should say sorry," I said.

"I am the teacher. I cannot possibly be accused of being rude when simply enforcing rules," she replied.

Right here is when I got in trouble because I got super duper a million times mad and said what I was thinking. I put my hands on my hips, looked straight into her dead eyes, and said, "You were mean on purpose, and you are breaking the rules! I heard you say in the hallway that you dislike children. Maybe you cause us stress! How would you like to walk into the same building daily, knowing the people inside don't like you? Kids are smart. Jasper and I know when we are not wanted, and knowing we are not wanted causes stress that makes our insides feel sick, and our brains cannot concentrate!"

Miss Hypo's face got as red as a crayon. She pointed toward the door, "Get out! Go to the front office, and I will deal with you later."

While I walked out with my fists balled up, she said, "Look, class. Nova needs to leave because Nova does not know how to follow the rules. She will be much happier when she learns to behave like a normal child and finally fit in."

I slowly turned toward her and snapped, "I don't know what you mean by a normal child because everyone in this class is different. No two are alike! During math class, you said you cannot put two different things into the same group. Remember? A fish is not a bird!" I screamed at the end of my sentence because I wanted to be heard. Mr. Pip says a person can be heard without screaming or crying. But, sometimes, my voice takes off. And anyway, adults are never clear about how kids should behave if we want them to listen to us.

I knew that standing up for Jasper was right, but I also knew I should have spoken with more respect. Being respectful is hard when you are not being respected. Before I walked through the door, I turned my head and looked at him one last time. He smiled small and gave me a thumbs-up. I would get in trouble a super duper a million times if it meant that Jasper knew someone cared about him.

The real swell lady at the front office called Mr. Pip to pick me up. He could not because he was getting a check-up at the doctor's office. Mr. Pip has had a lot of appointments lately.

Astrid came to pick me up instead. Before we left the office, I told Astrid about what happened all in one big breath, and I almost forgot to breathe!

She hugged me and said, "There will always be those who try to snuff out your light. But we must not get mad at them because they live in a dark and sad place." I told Astrid that Miss Hypo should move to a new house. She laughed and hugged me again.

As we were leaving, Miss Hypo stormed in and told Astrid the whole story from her perspective, as if Astrid would agree. Miss Hypo was disappointed.

Astrid smiled the way she always does when trying to hold onto her patience and said, "Miss Hypo, I thank you for your thoroughness. And now, would you be so kind as to sit down while Nova tells me the same story from her perspective? She politely listened to you, and I think it is only fair for you to hear her. If a judge, jury, and gavel is what you want, then all evidence must be presented from both sides. Indeed, as a reasonable and intelligent woman, you understand the fair trial process."

"I am shocked that you would teach a child to disrespect their elders. You were taught better, I know. What would your father think?"

"Crissy Hypo, if you think that teaching and bullying are synonymous, then perhaps you might evaluate your chosen profession. Nor do I appreciate your attempts at shaming me into silence," Astrid said.

"I did not bully anyone!" Miss Hypo insisted.

"Me thinks thou doth protest too much. Did you or did you not tell Jasper that a real blue jay dies every time he chirps like one?

And did you or did you not prevent Nova from offering comfort to one of your students who stood in need?" Astrid asked.

"I will not be insulted by you, Miss Beeswax. You are as incorrigible as Nova."

"I don't think incorrigible means what you think it means. Or, better stated, I know that Nova is not who you assume her to be from the calloused and assumptive lenses that color your world. Good day!" Astrid smoothed her dress as always, spun on her heel, and we took the long way to her car so we wouldn't need to walk by Miss Hypo. People sure mention Astrid's dad a lot. I know I would have liked him.

I held Astrid's hand super duper a million times tight, "Astrid, I want to be like you when I grow up, except I do not want to sell flowers. I want to sell happiness! Then, I can sell it to Miss Hypo because she is a wretched woman. Remember how you taught me that word, wretched? Maybe she won't be so mean to Jasper if I sell her happiness. I could also sell it to Jasper's mom so she would be nicer to him. Why do some kids have lots of people who love them, and some kids don't? Mr. Pip told me that happiness cannot be sold, but I told him that he
buys lots of things that make him smile, and what makes you smile makes you happy, right? Selling flowers makes you happy, right?"

"First, regarding children in desperate need of the unconditional love they deserve, the source is a plague known as Selfishness. When adults put their desires in front of children's needs, the children always lose. They lose their self-worth, confidence, feelings of safety, and awe for the wonders around them. Furthermore. . ."

"Jasper doesn't have Selfishness," I interrupted.

Astrid smiled tenderly, "No, no, he does not. Neither do flowers, which is one of the reasons I find peace and happiness when surrounded by their many varieties in all their colorful splendor and meaning, and I want to share it with others. Have you ever seen the smile on someone's face when they receive a beautiful bouquet for no reason at all? Such a small act of kindness helps someone feel loved. So many people want to be loved, as you can see in your friend Jasper."

"So, if happiness is not for sale, why do you sell flowers that make people happy? You are confusing me."

"Do you know another thing that makes me happy? I love it when you ask questions and tell me when I am confusing you. Let's try again. Human beings need each other. So, we buy the things we want and need from a person or a company, or pay them to do something for us that we cannot do for ourselves. For example, I purchase my dresses because I cannot make them, and I pay a painter to paint my house because I do not have the time and am afraid of heights. So, I create and sell floral arrangements because sharing what I love makes me happy, but I cannot sell my happiness to someone else. Now, what do you love?"

"I love excitement!"

"Well, then, start there. Excitement makes you happy. What exciting things could you do for someone else?" Astrid asked right as we walked inside The Bee's Knees. She brought me some biscotti, hot chocolate, a pencil, and a piece of paper with "Nova's Great Ideas" written in cute letters at the top. Kids need an adult who thinks their ideas are great, even if they're just one person!

Nova's Great Ideas

• Birthday Boxes Full of Glitter and Presents
• Choose Your Adventure Dog Walking Services
• Explosion Cookies
• Chasing Butterflies
• Goat Riding
• Rearranging the Orange Traffic Cones by My House
• Stuffie Surgery
• Cat Haircuts

***

Jasper showed up as soon as I finished eating my snacks and making my list.

"Hi, Nova! What are you doing? Can I do it, too?"

"These are my Great Ideas!" I said and read them one by one.

When I finished, Astrid brought Jasper his favorite snack, chocolate chip chippers (that's Jasper's code for chocolate chip cookies), a pencil, and paper with "Jasper's Great Ideas" written in cute letters at the top.

Chronicle the Second

Hiya Everyone! It's me, Nova! Guess what? Mr. Pip bought me a new trampoline because he had knee surgery and thought me and my real swell friend Jasper needed to expend our energy nearer to home while he recovers. Expend means to use up.

Roland put together the trampoline, which took forever. I submitted my complaint to Mr. Pip, and he told me that the only thing I should say when someone helps me is thank you, because they are being kind out of the goodness of their heart. If people can do things out of the goodness of their heart, can they also do things out of the badness of their heart? How can I tell? I have a lot of questions. You can learn anything if you ask lots of questions! Astrid says that curiosity is the key to the love of learning and to never stop asking.

Sometimes me and Jasper put the sprinkler under the trampoline while we jump, and sometimes we ride our bikes or push my daughters in their stroller. Have I told you about my daughters? I have seven! They are my children, and I love them super duper a million times much! Before me and Jasper were friends he made fun of me. He said my children were only dolls and not real, and I was weird for thinking they were! My feelings were hurt, and Astrid told me to explain to him why he hurt my feelings when he made fun of me. So, I did. His eyes looked so sad, and he said he was sorry. We've been friends since.

My daughters like to go on rides in the stroller, but sometimes, they jump out and break their legs, even though I tell them to sit still and stop arguing. I bandage them up and put them in a bright pink wheelchair until they are all better. When two of them break their legs at the same time, they fight over the wheelchair until I separate them. They hate being put in the time-out trash bag, but that's their consequence for making bad choices. Being a mother can be exhausting, so I make them go to bed at 3:00 in the afternoon when they are having hard days. Sometimes, everyone needs a nap. That's what Mr. Pip says, and he sleeps every other minute!

Do you want to know something shocking? The kids in my class have disappearing imaginations! A few weeks ago, Miss Hypo told us that we would be having a show-and-tell. She explained that we could bring something important to us and tell the class why. She said we could bring anything we wanted as long as we found it on her list of approved items. Do you want to know what her list of approved items includes? None of them sounded particularly interesting for a show-and-tell affair, and I shall only mention three so you can get an idea. Particularly means higher than usual.

• Favorite gluten-free snack – I think gummy bears would have been a good option, or maybe marshmallows. Possibly potato chips or lollipops.

• Entertainment – This category is what Astrid calls non-specific because it has no real parameters or definitions. Anything could be entertaining to somebody, which means this is an excellent category for anything that doesn't fit anywhere else. Astrid says there is always a creative solution to get around ridiculous, imagination-stifling rules. Stifling means making one feel oppressed.

• Favorite science book from teacher-approved list – All the science books listed were about irrelevant studies conducted twenty years ago.

Mr. Pip told me that outdated information that insists on being the only information is usually incorrect information. He also said that we should question those in authority who try to keep people ignorant, especially under the guise of education. Ignorance means a lack of knowledge or information. So, I asked him why he still sent me to Miss Hypo's class if she was trying to keep me uneducated. Seems rather contradictory to me! He didn't say a word and started combing his bushy white mustache with his toy pony comb.

Since Miss Hypo's category of entertainment was non-specific, I brought two of my daughters, Lucia and Chrystal, because taking care of them is what I do in my free time. I hid them in a paper grocery bag that I stapled shut so Jude the Dude wouldn't peek inside and run off to tell Miss Hypo, who would definitely object.

Here is what happened at show-and-tell.

Miss Hypo stood from her desk after our thirty minutes of fill-in-the-blank worksheet time had passed. I was done twenty-two minutes before she stood up and asked for another worksheet, but, of course, she said no to me. Then, I asked for paper to draw on, and she said no. I would have used my unicorn sketchbook, but she made a new rule that no sketchbooks were allowed in her classroom. Any necessary sketching would be accommodated by school-provided paper.

How does she have the authority to say whether sketching is or is not necessary? Why can't she just say that she doesn't like it and thinks art is a waste of time? That's what she said to one of the other teachers, the one who wears her hair in beautiful braids every day and speaks to her students with love. Sometimes, her braids change colors. One month, she had bubblegum pink braids, and the next month, she had blue jay-colored braids. Hair can tell you a lot about a person. Maybe that's why Miss Hypo decided she didn't like me the second she looked at me; my hair is art!

Anyway, after she stood up, she cleared her throat like she had been choking on pudding, smiled her fake smile, looked down her nose, and said, "Well, class, we have come to the most exciting part of the day! Show-and-tell. I am excited to learn more about each of you and trust that you followed my guidelines. Jasper will start, and we will move down the list until we reach the last person. Nova, that's you. We may not have time for everyone, and that's okay. We'll pick up where we left off next time we have show-and-tell. Before we begin, I must impress upon your mind the importance of respect. We do not tease or laugh at the interests of others. We do not ask rude questions. We do not judge. Jasper, please."

She waved her hand toward the stool and small table she had moved in front of the room. Miss Hypo's blonde hair reminds me of Mr. Pip's lederhosen after he irons it, straight and stiff. Sometimes, when she gets too close to my face, I can tell she uses a lot of makeup to cover up freckles, that her hair is the same brown as Astrid's chocolates, and that her contact lenses are a different color than her natural eyes. I wonder why she tries so hard to look like someone different. Maybe she thinks fitting in is a good thing, when really it leaves you looking and acting like a pretend version of yourself.

What happens when the rules for fitting in change?

Jasper's spirit won't let him fit in, even though he used to try. He said it was more difficult than talking in front of a classroom! We spent a long time working on his show-and-tell presentation because he gets so nervous. After we discussed what he would share for two entire hours, he finally chose to bring his favorite cardinal stuffy, Sharp Beak.

I could see his knees and hands shaking as he walked to the front of the room. When he got to the table he looked at the floor for a second, heard me whistle a C sharp like we planned, smiled, and raised his chin a little bit. Then, he bravely held his hands straight out in front of him with Sharp Beak standing on his palms. "Hi. This is my favorite stuffy. He's a cardinal, and I like cardinals. One interesting fact about cardinals is that they are the state bird for seven U.S. states: Illinois, Indiana, Kentucky, North Carolina, Ohio, Virginia, and West Virginia.

They are cute, and I love them," he said as he hugged Sharp
Beak.

We glanced sideways at Miss Hypo, waiting to see if she would
say or do something mean. Thankfully, she gave Jasper a nod
and a smile. But then ruined everything by saying, "Thank you,

Jasper, for sharing with us. Cardinals are indeed beautiful birds.
Next time, please be sure to abide by the guidelines I handed
out, or I will not be able to let you share."

Jasper started to smile as Miss Hypo began talking, but he was
hanging his head by the time she finished. I saw her smirk as she
watched him sit down. I think she did that out of the badness of
her heart. Also, Jasper technically abided by the guidelines since
studying birds and playing with bird toys are two ways Jasper
entertains himself.

Jude the Dude was next and talked about his favorite first-
person shooter video game. So did the next kid and the next.
Miss Hypo clapped a lot for each of them, saying they were so
lucky to have found something that took the burden of
pretending off their mind. She said pretending leads to hopes
for things that will never be, and we will be disappointed for the
rest of our lives.

Then, a boy named Leo took his turn. Leo is from a country in
Africa called Ethiopia. He is tall and has black curly hair, even
curlier than mine, and long black eyelashes. He unrolled a
poster he had drawn of his favorite snake, the coastal taipan.

Leo spoke until he was interrupted: "A taipan is a highly
venomous snake that lives in Australia and New Guinea. The
coastal taipan can grow up to ten feet long. All taipans have
neurotoxic venom, which affects the nervous system and can
cause paralysis."

"Thank you, Leo. I think we have heard quite enough about that
snake. While your knowledge is admirable, I trust that you, too,
will abide by the guidelines I gave you next time."

Leo raised an eyebrow as his arm, holding up his poster, dropped to his side, "Taipans are part of the study of reptiles. It's science."

"Yes, Leo, I know what science is, thank you, but this information did not come from one of the approved science books. However, you have brought before us a picture that may make another student feel unsafe and possibly threatened by the imposing look in the reptile's eyes. You would not want other students having nightmares because of the picture you drew, would you? I should think not. Now, please sit down without another word," Miss Hypo said, hissing like a snake at the end of the word, please.

Most of the kids laughed. Leo's face turned red, and he hung his head as well. After that, a couple more kids talked about video games and movies, and I was super duper a million times bored.

Mary Beth, a shy girl from India with beautiful wavy black hair, was the last person to share before it was my turn. I saw her holding something behind her back as she made her way to the front of the room. When she faced the class, she started breathing fast and looked scared. She glanced at Miss Hypo for help, but all Miss Hypo did was smile her wretched smile and say, "Just go with the guidelines, dear, and all will be well."

Mary Beth nodded, put whatever she held behind her back in her pocket, hung her head, and said that her brother likes to play the same game as Jude the Dude. I noticed the bright light in her eyes dim. She seems very kind and interesting, so me and Jasper plan on asking her to play with us. Leo, too. Astrid said we could host a lemonade party in her backyard to get to know each other.

Finally, it was my turn. "Nova, it's your turn. You have a minute or so before the bell rings," Miss Hypo instructed.

"The bell rings in fifteen minutes. I can tell time on your clock," I said as I marched to the front of the room with my two daughters.

Miss Hypo forced an annoyed smile, "You are correct, Nova. I must not have looked closely enough. You may proceed." I knew she knew exactly what time it was and hoped I couldn't tell the time on her special analog clock.

Mr. Pip has cuckoo clocks all over his house, so I learned real quick about the clocks' hands keeping track of time. Mr. Pip believes that all cuckoo clocks not made in the traditional style are an abomination. Do you know that word? Abomination? An abomination is something extremely offensive, disgusting, or morally wrong. When I asked him if the modern cuckoo clocks were extremely offensive, disgusting, or morally wrong, he said yes.

As I was opening my paper bag, Miss Hypo let out a big sigh, folded her arms over her chest, and cocked her head to the right. I tried to ignore her badness and talked anyway. "I am showing all of you my biggest treasure. These are two of my seven daughters, Lucia and Chrystal. Lucia loves Don, who doesn't love her back. She also sprays sushi and mayonnaise all over the walls. Chrystal doesn't love Don, but he loves her. Chrystal pukes all the time! Don is a purple bear with a big red heart on his foot. Lucia sent out wedding invitations for her and Don, even though Don never asked her to get married. They are way, way too into romance."

Jasper raised his hand, "Tell them about Chrystal of Life!"

Miss Hypo held up her hand, "Nova, do you seriously believe these dolls are real? You are seven and should know better. How could you have children? Right, class?"

Jude the Dude started laughing and pointing his finger at me, and pretty soon, most of the class was, too. Jasper stood up, "Miss Hypo told us not to laugh at or judge each other. Stop laughing at Nova!"

Miss Hypo kept rocking forward and back on her shiny black high heels, laughing until she cried while repeating, "Nova thinks she has daughters! I knew that child had problems." Her laugh was not happy sounding.

Because everyone but Jasper, Leo, and Mary Beth were laughing at me, I got super duper a million times sad. But I refused to hang my head and cry. Instead, I put Chrystal and Lucia back in my bag, held my chin high, and returned to my seat. The bell took a bajillion years to ring, and I didn't hear anything else Miss Hypo said. I imagined sticking chewed-up bubble gum all over

her car and wrapping so much cotton candy around the tires that she would be stuck in sugar-glue until it rained. Astrid would call that thought an inside thought, so I kept it to myself and promised myself I would not be mean to someone who was mean to me.

Thankfully, when school got out, Astrid was there, ready to walk with me to The Bee's Knees. Everyone needs someone to walk with them. She had even brought my stroller, like I asked, so I could push my daughters as a reward for behaving on their field trip.

Astrid could tell I was having a rough time and asked, "Nova, whatever is the matter?"

 "Miss Hypo made fun of me during show-and-tell because I love my daughters. She said they were just dolls. Then, most of the other kids started laughing with her. Why were they laughing at me? I didn't laugh at their lack of imagination when I was super duper a million times bored!"

"Let me tell you a story, Nova. When I was in fourth grade, one of our regular assignments involved looking up vocabulary words in the dictionary. Most kids bemoaned the obligation, but I relished the opportunity to expand my mind. They teased me and called me a know-it-all. It hurts when people you think are your friends laugh at you. I'm so sorry."

"Well, I knew Jude the Dude was not my friend. Did you start keeping your love of the dictionary a secret?" I asked.

Astrid replied, "Golly gee, no! Why would I forfeit my education for the approval of others? If I had stopped, I would not be where I am today, and I would have given my power to people who did not care about me. Similarly, you must never forfeit your imagination because others would rather you be small and think small. They are free to shape their minds according to their desires and can afford you the same privilege. If a person demands that you give them freedom of expression while simultaneously demanding that you rid yourself of your individuality because they don't understand it, that's absurd."

"What does absurd mean?"

"Unreasonable, illogical, or ridiculous. It's unreasonable to give someone else power over your life. It's illogical to let their opinion override yours, and it's ridiculous to demand tolerance out of another when one is unwilling to extend such grace themselves. Now, put Lucia and Chrystal in their stroller, and let's be off. The Harvest Festival is six weeks away, and we have much to prepare. Additionally, you have writing assignments."

I quickly buckled my daughters into their seats, even though they were fighting over who got the front seat. "Do I get to write about Mr. Pip's knee surgery? How is he doing today? Did Roland check on him? Did you check on him?"

"If you write about Mr. Pip's knee surgery, what would you write?"

"Hmmm. I would probably write about the side effects of surgery they don't tell you about," I answered.

"Oh, and what are those?" Astrid asked.

I explained, "For one, Mr. Pip is now boring. He used to sing and smile all the time, and now he just looks sad. For two, Mr. Pip has lost his sense of humor. He doesn't make jokes or laugh at mine. All he does is say that he wants to close his eyes for a minute and then closes them for hours."

"When someone you love cannot do what they normally do, it can be a hard adjustment. However, Mr. Pip had the surgery so his knee would be stable again, and with his physical recovery will come the recovery of his sense of humor and energy. I assure you, in a year, this will be a memory. In the meantime, you get to come with me to The Bee's Knees, jump on your trampoline with Jasper, eat a lot of good food, and otherwise have a wonderful time. I know Mr. Pip would feel loved if you did something thoughtful for him. Remember when you were sick with the flu, and he cared for you?" Astrid asked.

"I remember," I answered. She had a good point. I was very sick and got so sad when I couldn't get out of bed, go outside, or go anywhere else. When Mr. Pip, Jasper, and Astrid had things to do simultaneously, I got even sadder because I was all alone by myself! Simultaneously means at the same time.

"I could make him cookies, draw him a picture, write him a story, sing him a song, or look through his old pictures while he tells me stories," I offered. Then I thought a little longer, "What do you think? What part of your brain is the thinking part? Does it get bigger as you get older? Does everyone have a thinking brain? Mr. Pip's dog Odin does not have a thinking brain; I can tell you that," I said.

Odin eats dirt and bites his own tail. He also swallowed an entire squirrel one time. The entire squirrel in one gulp!

"I think, sometimes, people who are not feeling well simply want the people they love around them. Perhaps you could sit with him and read one of the stories you have written for him? He is a good listener. Did you know he was a dentist before he retired?" Astrid asked.

"Yes, he told me I could use his old dental tools to clean my daughter's teeth if I wanted. Maybe he could watch me be a dentist. Do you think he would like that?"

"He would be honored," Astrid said, and I knew she was telling the truth because her eyes and smile matched.

So, that's what I did. I brought down all seven of my daughters and set them up in a row facing Mr. Pip. After I put on my purple latex gloves, I laid them down one by one and got the sugar bugs off their teeth. I also had to break up fights and give them candy.

Mr. Pip's knee is so swollen that it looks like a baby's head is coming out of it. That's super duper a million times gross, right? I didn't get sad when he fell asleep because I could tell his knee hurt. When he woke up, he suggested I wash the pen marks off my daughters ' arms and faces so they could be clean. I had to explain that they were in a tattoo war last week and kept drawing tattoos on each other with permanent markers. I tried to stop them, but they wouldn't listen. Now, they must bathe, and I will be forced to listen as they fight over the bubbles! Being a mother really is exhausting. Thankfully, I have Jasper to help me. We will plan our lemonade party with Leo and Mary Beth when he comes over later. I'll tell you how the party went next time!

Show and Tell

Chronicle the Third

Hiya Everyone! It's me, Nova. Mr. Pip has been a humongous grump lately. I asked, "Mr. Pip! Do you want to jump off the roof onto the trampoline with me? We could buy party balloons to keep us from falling too quickly."

"No, Nova. No one is jumping off the roof today or any other day, and regretfully, I must tell you that party balloons for the purpose of breaking nature's law of gravity only work in movies."

I did not like how he didn't smile or how his bushy white mustache hadn't been combed after breakfast. That's an entire two hours, and the longest I have seen him go without getting out his tiny pony comb is maybe seventeen minutes! Plus, he didn't tell me he appreciated my imagination, even if my ideas were not practicable.

So, I said, "Mr.Pip! You are boring me! You have lost your sense of humor!" He said, "Mmmhmm," and leaned his head back.

Me and Jasper told Astrid what was happening to her oldest friend and that she had better fix him fast before he ruined my life.

"Mr. Pip has not lost his sense of humor, nor is he ruining your life. He is recovering from knee surgery and is in a lot of pain. Pain can be rather demanding and rob one of their cheery outlooks for a season, like a thief who breaks in and steals the lights in your house. I assure you, the lights always come back in one way or another. Be patient and be kind," Astrid patted our heads as she spoke.

Why do adults pat kids on the head? After I was done being a super duper million times frustrated with Mr. Pip for getting old, me and Jasper decided to find the thief who took his sense of humor and get it back if it's not returned in a week or two.

We think Miss Hypo is the thief, but it may be someone else. Jasper marked the date on his calendar so we can remember it. We cannot do it right now because we are adventuring. You cannot do two things at once and do them both well. That's what Mr. Pip says. I bet there are people in this whole wide world who come close. Mr. Pip told me not to assume that I am one of those people because I have difficulty focusing on even one thing. He is not entirely correct because I am super duper a million times good at focusing on my art and my friends.

Me and Jasper have made two new friends, Leo and Mary Beth. Remember them from my class? I will tell you about each of them. Mary Beth has a big smile and bigger dimples. She takes ballet classes three times a week and writes a lot of letters. I think she's shy, but Astrid said she thinks Mary Beth is socially cautious and wants to know the unspoken rules of the company she keeps before engaging. I don't understand why unspoken rules matter one hoot.

If she starts playing with me and Jasper all the time, she might want to learn to talk whenever she wants. We don't have waiting lines. Oh, and she loves dogs. Crocus, Astrid's dog, loved her immediately. Good thing Crocus doesn't care about unspoken social rules.

Leo knows a lot about snakes, sharks, and dinosaurs. He knows as much about them as Jasper knows about birds. He says his brain and mouth don't always work together because words get switched around and garbled unless he is talking about snakes, sharks, and dinosaurs. He likes to draw pictures of them, but he says the part of his brain that jumbles his words jumbles his hands; they won't cooperate! Leo also told me that he has a condition known as Hard Hands. Hard Hands press down too hard on pencils, pens, and paintbrushes.

I told him that enjoying a hobby is a good enough reason to do it. Astrid told me that if she stacked all her failures next to all her successes, I might find the first far outweighed the second.

Since Astrid loves decorating for parties, she has all sorts of supplies at her house. We used them to make and mail Leo and Mary Beth an invitation with a glittery killer whale on the front and a formal request for their response, commonly known as an RSVP, which represents a French term that means, 'Please respond.'

Me and Jasper also shoved a bunch of rainbow sprinkles in each envelope in case Leo or Mary Beth needed something sweet. Sweet treats seem to help people feel better. Mary Beth responded affirmatively with a letter by post. Affirmatively is a new word I learned. It means expressing agreement or consent. So, Mary Beth agreed to come to our party.

Leo, being shy, didn't say anything until Jasper asked him. Leo said his mom said he could come, but he couldn't decide if he wanted to go until he found out what we were celebrating. Jasper told him we were having a party just for fun. Leo said he had never heard of such a thing, but decided to come because he thought he might discover some new creature in a backyard other than his own.

When the day of the party arrived, Jasper's dad dropped him off at my house at 7:30 am. Jasper's dad always smiles and teases us. Plus, he never calls me Nova. Instead, he calls me Georgina! He's a joker and the only person in this whole wide world allowed to call me anything but Nova. Nova is my name, and I like it.

I asked Jasper why his mom yells at him so much if she is married to a kind man. He shrugged his shoulders and said, "She says sorry every Sunday and promises to try again."

"She doesn't seem to know how to keep promises!"

"I try to do a lot of things, and I still don't do them very well. I think yelling is like that for her," Jasper said.

"But she makes you hang your head and cry! She should try harder," I was beginning to get rather irritated. I almost stomped my foot!

"She makes herself cry more. I hear her tell my dad how bad she feels for losing her temper when she thinks me and my sisters are asleep. People are people, and people are weird," he whispered, shrugging his shoulders before becoming a chicken.

He always transforms into a chicken when he doesn't know what to do with himself. He scratches the ground with his feet, flaps his elbows behind his back like he has wings, and screams "ba-cluck, ba-cluck," super duper a million times loud.

We asked Mr. Pip if we could have leftover apple pie for breakfast. Usually, he would say no, but he said yes with a chuckle. After we ate our pie, we played Stuffydom for a few hours until Astrid came to the door and told us it was time to get ready for our lemonade party. We love to play Stuffydom, but I will tell you about that later because it gets complicated—very complicated. My daughters are way too into romance.

I opened the door before Astrid could knock. "Hiya, Astrid! Did you buy the edible glitter that I asked for? Are we going to use big or little cups? Did your mom agree to let us use the tea set she got from her grandma? Remember, I promised we wouldn't break it or use it for paintbrush water. Did you bring strawberries? Did you get art supplies? Do we get to use your fancy umbrellas?" I had so many questions! It's a good thing Astrid is accustomed to my curiosity.

Jasper stood behind me and turned into a loud chicken again. Astrid politely put her finger in her left ear as she squeezed her eyes shut and wrinkled her nose. "Jasper, my dear, wonderful Jasper. You make such an adorable chicken, and I wonder if you could pretend to be the quietest chicken in the world for today."

Jasper grinned, and his scratching feet became as quiet as a cats, and his ba-cluck was hardly a whisper. Astrid rewarded him with a big smile and a pat on his fuzzy blonde head. Since Jasper can only be quiet for a few minutes when we are playing at my house, I knew we needed to run outside, where our noise gets absorbed by the clouds.

Astrid followed us, looking beautifully. I want to look like her when I grow up. She wore a lemon-yellow dress with a big bow on the back. "Nova, Jasper, come along. Your guests will arrive soon, and you must be ready. Rule number one when it comes to conducting business is respecting people's time."

"But Astrid, we are not conducting business. We are just having our friends over for a lemonade party," I protested.

"If you must respect others when conducting business, what does that teach you about how you should treat your friends?" she asked.

"Treat them better, better, better!" Jasper said, between hopping on one foot and naming the birds that flew overhead.

Astrid winked, smoothed her dress, spun on her heel, and walked toward her back porch, "Here we have a round table for lemonade, cucumber and cream cheese sandwiches, and chips. Before you ask, there will be dessert. Strawberry shortcake, as requested. Over yonder by the flowering magenta and purple asters, we have reserved the rectangular table for crafts. Will you two please do me a favor? Will you retrieve the paper bags of art supplies by the sliding glass door? Nova, you might find the answers to some of your questions in those bags."

Me and Jasper raced to the door and dragged out the heavy paper bags. Astrid had two white tablecloths. One was covered with colorful butterflies and daffodils, while the other had snakes and rocks. We decided the butterfly one belonged on the eating table and the snake one belonged on the art table. She also bought plastic cups with lemons and bumblebees, matching paper plates, napkins, and bowls.

For the art table, we had glitter galore: popsicle sticks, sequins, construction paper, strings, and stickers! Astrid explained these were all intended as decorative options for the little wooden birdhouses she found at Not Your Grandma's Doily Yarn and Lace. I want the entire Not Your Grandma's Doily Yarn and Lace for Christmas!

I organized the supplies, and Jasper helped cut the strawberries for our dessert. Then we helped Astrid blow up the balloons for our yellow and white balloon arch! We put the arch and a welcome sign in the front yard with Mary Beth and Leo's names, and we were ready for our special guests.

Leo came early. He scanned the backyard from side to side, turned to Jasper, who had turned into a chicken again, and asked, "Have you seen any venomous snakes today? Not so much venomous snakes live in our geographical range."

"Nope! Ba-cluck!" Jasper said.

"Chickens sometimes eat small snakes," Leo observed.

Jasper turned around, ran, and yelled, "Chicken fight!"

At the word fight, Leo bent his elbows, brought his hands to his chest, and roared like a dinosaur. Off he ran, not after Jasper, but in a random pattern, gnashing his teeth at something imaginary.

A few minutes later, Mary Beth arrived in an elegant pink dress, black on top, with a fluffy pink tutu and pink ballet slippers. She had a white purse draped across her body with a zipper on top, and pink silk flowers on the strap. I wonder if anyone has asked her if she used to be a porcelain doll. "Hiya, Mary Beth. How are you doing on this real swell day? Are you excited to have a lemonade party? We have all sorts of exciting art projects. Well, technically, we have one art project with a lot of different options. Astrid believes in having options."

"Hello, Nova. Thank you for inviting me to your party. Do you truly call your mother by her first name?" Mary Beth asked, tilting her head and furrowing her brow.

"No! Astrid is not my mother. She is my friend. I live next door with my great uncle, Mr. Pip. His first name is Charles, but he says that Uncle Charles could be turned into Uncle Chuck, which could turn into Uncle Chuckles, and nobody wants an Uncle Chuckles. So, he says that calling him Mr. Pip is perfectly acceptable."

"Where is your mother?" Mary Beth asked.

Just then, Astrid came swooping in with two pitchers of lemonade and sang out, "Welcome, welcome, my four special guests. Each of you can find your place at the table; a name card is in front of your plate."

Sure enough, Astrid had written our names in swirly letters and clipped them to mint leaves. I was glad she came when she did because I did not want to tell Mary Beth about my mother or my father.

Astrid explained, "I will be your server. Atop your plate, you will find a menu. There are three types of sandwiches to choose from and three types of chips. On the bottom, you will find a selection of fruits and vegetables. Choose three from each. The portions are small, and if you are not yet satiated after you consume your portions, seconds are on the house. You may order your meal by circling the pictures of the food of your choosing. I will return in ten minutes, and until then, please enjoy either pure lemonade or raspberry lemonade, along with cucumbers and goldfish."

"Wow, Astrid! I didn't know you would make a menu," I said.

Jasper screamed, and Leo smiled and examined his hands.

Mary Beth said, "Thank you," in a quiet voice. I wonder if she ever has Scream Attacks.

After Astrid brought us our food, I got down to business. "So, Leo and Mary Beth, do you want to be friends with me and Jasper? We have a real swell time together. Leo, you can talk about snakes whenever you want, and Mary Beth, you can do whatever you like, and no one will make fun of either of you. That's a pretty good deal, I think. What do you say?"

"I would love to be your friend," Mary Beth said as she smiled her big dimple smile.

Leo didn't say anything for what seemed like forever. "Well, Leo? What do you say?" I asked.

"He cannot think right now because he is being fully weaponized," Jasper explained.

"No, no. I cannot be weaponized right now. I can think, but sometimes, the right words don't get on top of my head, " Leo said.

"That's okay, Leo." Mary Beth said while patting his hand.

"I, I don't like to be touched," he said, pulling his hand back.

"I am so sorry, Leo!" Mary Beth's eyes started to water.

"That, that's okay. You didn't know. I want to be your friend. I just don't like to be touched by anyone except my mom. My mom can hug me, but only if she asks first, because sometimes, I am not in a hugging mood. I don't like surprise hugs, either," Leo kept staring at his hands or glancing over his left shoulder as he spoke.

In fact, now that I think of it, he didn't look anyone in the eye for the entire party! I wonder why. I'll need to ask him later.

We were quiet as we scarfed down our dessert. When we finished, we went to the craft table.

Leo spoke again, "Mary Beth, I have been wondering what you planned to share during Show and Tell. What was it?"

"I want to know what it was, too! I knew you didn't plan on sharing that your brother likes the video game the others were talking about," I added.

"Dear me, I was hoping no one saw it. Did you see me hiding something, too, Jasper?"

"Ba-cluck!" He said with a head nod.

Mary Beth smiled, unzipped her purse, and brought out a tiny light blue dolphin, crocheted with what must be the tiniest needles in the world. "What I am about to share with you is very, very special. It represents my hobby, and my hobby brings me happiness. It's true that I didn't want Miss Hypo to get upset with me, but more than that, I didn't want her, or the class, to make fun of what I love. People don't always deserve to know what makes you special when they don't know how to care for special things. My mother tells me that all the time."

"So, you love dolphins?" Leo asked.

"Yes! And I love to crochet small animals," she explained.

"You mean you like to crochet small versions of big animals. The biggest member of the dolphin family is the orca, commonly known as the killer whale. According to my favorite educational public programming television station, the largest male orca on record was 32 feet long and 22,000 pounds. The most common dolphin, the bottlenose dolphin, is not so big as the orca, but still weighs between 180 and 330 pounds. On average."

 A pause lasting a thousand years followed, and I worried that Mary Beth got her feelings hurt. Instead, she started laughing, and then I was worried that Leo would get his feelings hurt.

"Why are we laughing?" asked Jasper, who had long since started opening every glitter package with at least half the glitter falling in the grass.

The wasted glitter almost made me super duper a million times mad because I had a lot of plans for it, but I decided to follow Roland's advice. He said that fights over cheap things are not worth hurting a friend. I don't know how much glitter costs, but I've heard Astrid say it's one of the most inexpensive ways to make something look fancy.

Mary Beth interrupted my ruminations over the ruined art supplies by letting out a laughing snort, "I'm sorry, Leo, I am not laughing at you. I am laughing because my father told me the same thing, and I forgot. Thanks for reminding me!"

"You're welcome," Leo said.

"Let's get started on your birdhouses, shall we?" Astrid asked as she came, sweeping in like a graceful broom to clean the table.

"What do you all think about decorating a house for Miss Hypo? Teacher Appreciation Day is coming up, and I think a thoughtful gesture would touch her heart."

"I don't appreciate her at all," I said.

"I don't think she has a heart," Leo added.

Jasper made a peregrine falcon's piercing and high-pitched cry, "kak-kak-kak!"

Mary Beth said nothing, but I did see her roll her eyes.

Astrid held up a large birdhouse, complete with a little door, "I know she is not kind, thoughtful, or even approachable, and she does so on purpose. She certainly does not deserve to know what makes you special if she cannot see it already. However, she is your teacher, and you can show her that beauty can be created when people work together. You will have a grand time turning this birdhouse into a masterpiece, no matter who you give it to, so why not her? You are simply sharing something pretty with her, not giving her a Teacher of the Year award."

I crinkled my nose, stuck out my tongue, and folded my arms, "Miss Hypo-pot-a-mus is super duper a million times rude!"

Astrid smiled again and rubbed my back, "So is making fun of her last name. Remember, how you treat others says much more about you than it does about them."

Jasper asked if we could fill the birdhouse with nocturnal spiders that attack people in their sleep, and Astrid told him that was not very nice either.

In the end, we each decorated one side of the birdhouse in whatever way we wanted: snakes, chickens, dolphins, and bright circles with cat faces in the middle.

Astrid wrote a card, which she bribed us all to sign by giving us a bag of gummy bears.

After putting the house in a gift bag covered with spring flowers, she handed us pinwheels, Mason jars, and a magnifying glass, "Go play and discover! Thank you for trying to be nice, even though you didn't want to."

We ran off before Astrid had any more ideas about Miss Hypo. Mary Beth didn't run, though; she did ballerina leaps instead.

Speaking of Miss Hypo, she said a phrase I've never heard before: "stop at nothing."

I don't know what else she said, but I am just wondering—what does "stop at nothing" mean? Is there a place called Nothing where some people stop to get a snack, and some people don't? Who wouldn't want to stop for a snack?

Mary Beth and Leo are now part of my patchwork family.

Leo is my science patch because he knows so much about dinosaurs, snakes, and sharks. Everyone needs a science patch to ensure accuracy and simplify complex information.

Mary Beth is my ballet patch because she loves ballet and practices a lot of self-control. She's a good example of how to solve problems without kicking and screaming.

Chronicle the Fourth

Hiya, Everyone! It's me, Nova. I just had the scariest Halloween in this whole big wide world! Halloween is my fourth favorite holiday. My other favorite holidays are Father's Day, Christmas, and Easter. Sometimes, holidays two and three switch places on my favorites list, but numbers one and four always stay the same.

Father's Day is my favorite holiday because I was born on Father's Day, and it was the best present my dad could have asked for, basically. I like to remember that my dad had red hair like me. My hair helps me remember my mama, too. Her hair was even bigger than mine!

Mama was an exciting woman. Mr. Pip says so. Her clothes rarely matched, and she talked fast while making wild hand gestures. She lost all kinds of things in her hair, like my whistles, kazoos, and permanent markers. Why are adults always trying to take permanent markers away from children?

When she got sick, she stopped talking fast, then started talking slow, then stopped talking altogether. But I could still bring a smile to her face when I gave her Mama Hugs, and before she died, she wrote me a letter saying my Mama Hugs kept her going, and she couldn't wait until she held me again. I wonder when that will be?

When I ask Mr. Pip, he pauses for a long time, lets out a big breath, and says, "Well," before stumbling over his words.

Why is it hard to say, "I don't know?" And why do people get embarrassed when they cry?

Me and Jasper cried when we got scared while trick-or-treating with our new friends. Remember them? Mary Beth, and Leo? I dressed up as a basket of laundry. Jasper went as a cardinal, of course. Mary Beth dressed up as an electric shock, and Leo went as a Burmese python with a stuffed deer attached to the top of his head because Burmese pythons are known to eat entire deer.

Did you know they have heat-sensing pits? It's true. The pits are located along their upper jaw, and they help them detect warm-blooded prey. You probably know that humans have armpits that make smells. That's what Leo taught me. He taught me a super duper million times lots of things during our Halloween adventures.

Every year Doily Dayle decorates Spooktacular Lane on the block where The Bee's Knees and Oswald's Tiny Toys are located. Floating candles, flying bats, glowing pumpkins, and adults and kids wearing costumes of all kinds made me happy.

Astrid was dressed as a Victorian-era witch, stirring an enormous cauldron of candy she set up on the sidewalk. Her dress was black with long lace-trimmed sleeves, a lace-up corset, and tons and tons of dark purple tulle. She had black and orange roses all over her witch hat and fake crow feathers, which Jasper did not appreciate. She wore high lace-up boots made from black leather. Roland told me she has worn those boots every Halloween for twenty years. Maybe they remind her of someone special.

Next to the cauldron, Astrid set up a craft table where kids could make ghosts out of tissue paper and lollipops or latex gloves to make scary hands by using Smarties for the fingers and chocolate for the rest. Jasper said there were too many kids at the table when we walked by, so we scurried over to Oswald's Tiny Toys, where Oswald was handing out caramel apples drizzled in chocolate and dipped in crushed toffee.

He wore his usual Kelly green cable knit sweater with a giant black exclamation point made out of construction paper taped to the front.

"I don't understand your costume," Leo observed.

"I've recently been accused of talking in exclamation points, so I thought I might walk around wearing one and see how I faired," Oswald explained with a click of his heels and a chuckle.

Leo raised an eyebrow, "The fair was three months ago."

"No, no, dear child. This is a joke. You see ..."

Leo shook his head, "I am not so good at understanding jokes."

"My, but you are a clever boy, aren't you? You are wearing a snake costume with a stuffed deer on your head to clarify that you are a Burmese python rather than another snake," Oswald kindly pointed out.

"Burmese pythons eat deer. Snakes' jaws are connected by an elastic ligament, and human jaws are connected by a bone, so the deer on my head is for illustrative educational purposes," Leo said, raising his eyebrow even higher.

"You are both so smart!" Mary Beth said as Oswald and Jasper tried to figure out what to say next.

People shift when they are uncomfortable, I've noticed. Their feet shift, their eyes shift, and their hands shift from their elbows to their shoulders and back.

"Trick-or-treat!" Jasper yelled, holding out his Cheep-Cheep Birdy Halloween bag that looked like a bird's nest. Sharp Beak was inside.

Jasper had not been paying attention to our conversation since there were so many colorful and clinking distractions. Sometimes, I get super duper a million times annoyed with

Jasper because he doesn't pay attention, and when he doesn't pay attention, I feel like he doesn't care. Astrid assures me that Jasper is a wonderful friend who needs my patience as he manages his struggles. Astrid doesn't understand that Jasper's inability to pay attention is more my struggle than his!

In the middle of Jasper making a ruckus, Jude the Dude appeared with his friends from Camping Club. Ruckus means a disturbance or commotion. They were dressed up bears. All five of them. Same costume. No deviation. What a snooze fest.

"Hey, look! It's Flame Brain Nova and Jiggly Wigs Jasper," he teased.

"No, sir, not in my shop," Oswald said as he peered over his glasses and pointed to a white and green sign on the wall. "If your feet are planted on my property, you will respect my rule."

Oswald's one rule was this: Do and say only that from which good will come.

Jude the Dude read the sign and smirked, "Laughing makes me feel good, and I like to laugh at Nova because she's an easy target."

Right here is where I got a super duper a million times mad, so I clenched my fists and screamed until Jude the Dude covered his ears and ran down to Astrid's cauldron. She had heard me screaming, of course, and used her powers of observation to answer her own questions. I hoped she would refuse to give him candy, but she gave him the exact amount she gave everyone else. How annoying!

"Oh, bless us, dear child. I don't think much good comes from screaming; it's a wonder the glass in the windows didn't explode," Oswald said.

I sighed a heavy sigh, "Good did come of my screaming because Jude the Dude left! I don't like him, and I would be so happy if I never, ever, never, ever, ever see his mean face again. I should call him Jude the Rude Dude and see how he likes it. Leo, does he make fun of you?"

"He tried once while we were at the library, but I told him I only speak snake and went back to my book," Leo said.

"What did he say to you?" Jasper asked as he picked up tiny toys, only to have Oswald gently take them out of his hand and put them back on the shelf.

"I don't remember because I don't care. I recall reading a book about black mambas, some of the fastest and most venomous snakes in the world. They can reach speeds up to twelve miles an hour, and black mambas are not truly black. Their skin is usually gray or dark brown," Leo said.

"Hmph. That's not fair. If I told him I only speak snake, he would still tease and tattle on me," I said.

"You don't know enough about snakes to speak snake," Leo said as he unwrapped a lollipop and stuck it in his mouth.

"Leo, you don't understand my plight because you don't have it. Mary Beth, does he make fun of you?" I asked.

"No, but he once pulled the pink satin bow out of my hair. So, I pulled the sack lunch from his hand and told him that he could have his lunch when he gave me back my bow," Mary Beth answered.

"Really? What happened after that?" Jasper asked, setting down the tiny toy in his hands and giving Mary Beth his full attention.

"Yeah, what happened?" Me and Leo exclaimed.

"He gave me back my bow, and I gave him back his lunch. That's it," Mary Beth said with a shrug.

"Children, dear children. Let's not give Jude the Dude the power to spoil the rest of Halloween. You still have plenty of stops to make along Spooktacular Lane. Now, run along," Oswald instructed as his hands and fingers danced us down the sidewalk.

We obeyed, and after trick-or-treating at Doily Dayle Books and Not Your Grandma's Doily Yarn and Lace, we arrived at a boring store, Supplies for the End. The supplies they have for sale are canned food, first-aid kits, sleeping bags, tarps, heavy boots, and binoculars. The only kinds of candy they have are bags of lemon drops and horehound. Horehound is super duper a million times gross, and I wouldn't waste your money. It's an herb root that's been around at least as long as ancient Egypt and tastes like bitter dirt with sugar on top.

Astrid says the shop's owner is a cranky old coot named Yabutiah Itsasham. (His name is pronounced Yeah-but-I-uh It's-a-sham. Astrid says it sounds like the beginning of an excuse). He thinks the world is ending and believes that celebrations of any sort hasten our inevitable destruction.

I asked why he participates in Spooktacular Lane if he believes celebrations are wrong, and Astrid said he excels at fear-based marketing. She also says he has a bee in his bonnet about everything. He could not leave the Halloween celebrators to themselves if he tried. No, he had to point out the dangers of candy consumption upon the teeth and brain, explain why kids in costumes eventually became rioters, and theorize that the blatant disrespect for bats and pumpkins would incur nature's wrath next week by his educated estimation. I think he wants a hug, but doesn't know how to say the words. Sometimes, people's mouths won't let them say the thoughts deep inside their hearts, so they spew out crankiness instead.

Before we reached old Yabutiuh's table, we watched Miss Crissy Hypo walk into Supplies for the End with a large canvas bag and enormous sunglasses, which would not have been suspicious had she been wearing a costume. But, since she had no costume, she was very suspicious because she doesn't usually wear enormous sunglasses or carry big bags. You can't be sneaky and obvious at the same time!

"Stop! There is Miss Hypo. Should we find out what she is doing in there?" I whispered.

"We might get in trouble if we go inside," Mary Beth pointed out.

"Trouble? What trouble?" Jasper asked.

"Well, someone might get mad at us. And, if Miss Hypo sees us, she will be mad for the rest of the year and make our lives difficult just because she can," Mary Beth said.

"She already does that," Leo said.

"We aren't doing anything mean to her; we just want to hear what she's doing. We don't even need to see her," I said to soothe Mary Beth's fears.

"Astrid says that when you listen closely, people give away their secrets without realizing it. She says you must listen to what they say and what they do not say," I explained.

"Ba-cluck! Ba-cluck!" Within seconds, Jasper left our huddle and started bumping repeatedly into Yabutiah's table, bobbing and tilting his head, scratching the ground, and knocking down a bowl of hard candies— probably horehound and lemon drops.

"Stop it! Stop it! What is wrong with you? Are you dense?" the old man yelled. "Have your candy and be done with it! See what I mean, Charles? The children here are completely out of control. Look, now the bird boy is running into the wall."

"I do see that," Mr. Pip said as he slowly combed his bushy mustache with his toy comb. "I spent decades working with kids as a dentist, and I can tell you that their imaginations are much more interesting than our adult realities."

"We're safe. Mr. Pip will watch over us. Let's go," I whispered as we let the distraction hide our steps.

"Jasper's a genius," Leo said with a genuine smile.

"I know! He's waiting for the rest of us to catch up," Mary Beth whispered back as we hurried along.

When we stepped inside Supplies for the End, we could hear voices in the back room, which was easy because the beige-colored linoleum floors amplified the sound.

Amplified comes from the word "amplify," which means to make something bigger.

We tiptoed through the aisles of shelves made of unfinished wood, where no decorations or exciting colors could be seen. No wonder Yabutiah thinks the world has no hope. His world has no art!

We instantly heard Miss Hypo talking with the same disdain in her voice that she uses when she teaches, "I came here to discuss the next steps for our education reform, and I was under the impression that such plans were completed, compiled, and deliverable upon receipt of payment. Here is my payment."

"Yes, you are correct. All is deliverable upon receipt of payment, which you have yet to produce," said a voice belonging to a super duper a million times old lady. I could tell she was old because her voice was low and crinkly.

"How much more money could someone like you possibly need?"

"Oh my. I believe you have been mistaken. Monetary payments are for commoners. No, no, Miss Hypo. When you make deals with me, you pay in favors and compromises, the conditions of which are set by me and not you. Do you understand?"

"I understand corruption if that is what you are hinting at."

The low and crinkly voice kept talking, "And yet here you are, asking to join our ranks and thinking you can simply for the wanting. The pungent aroma of your entitlement is enough to make one wish their olfactory senses were temporarily or permanently compromised, depending on how often one must endure your presence. Still, since Halloween is my favorite holiday, I can forgive your naivete this once. Nonetheless, I must make myself clear. Consenting to meet with us today confirmed that you care more about The Cause than yourself. As such, you will do what you are told to do without the slightest deviation and mind your manners."

"The Cause? I thought we were talking about education reform," Miss Hypo said, the anger fading from her voice. When anger fades from your voice it means your voice stops trying to hit people in the face.

"I think we should go," Mary Beth whispered. "I'm getting scared, and I think Miss Hypo is getting scared, too."

The rest of us nodded, but still we sat, frozen.

The old voice said to Miss Hypo, "We are. The two are enmeshed."

"Can I at least know the cause before I agree to sign over my soul?" Miss Hypo asked.

"Did you not hear me but two minutes ago, you daft girl? You've already signed the dotted line by showing up. Gus, did you or did you not make it clear to Crissy Hypo that once she met with me personally, she was fully committed?"

"I did," said a deep voice.

"You see, Crissy, we have your information. We are aware of your assets, bank accounts, internet service provider, and everything else. We are even aware of your compromises, which I don't believe you want to be made public. Oh, my, wait. I believe I have misspoken. We do not know everything about you. Our data collection has told us nothing about the people you love. No one visits your house, and no friends or family call or text you. No one can so much as move their thumbs for your benefit. How sad. I'm starting to think the only person that matters to you is … you. Am I right?"

"I'm not that selfish," Miss Hypo said.

"Miss Hypo is getting sad, and it sounds like she is hanging her head," Jasper said.

"I think we should leave here now!" Mary Beth whispered, louder this time.

"Besides, Crissy," the crinkly voice continued, "we are not asking you to do more than what you are already doing, for now. Please make your students feel small, stupid, and insignificant. So much so that the mere hint of a compliment will have them bending to your will. Approval, Miss Hypo. Students who seek approval at any cost are malleable. You will be in ultimate control of your classroom."

"No, she won't. The old lady will be in charge because she is in charge of Miss Hypo. She just said so," Leo pointed out.

"Let's do what Mary Beth says and leave," I said, and we scooted down the aisle toward the door. None of us wanted to hear how the conversation ended.

Once we got out, Jasper started crying, "I left my Cheep-Cheep bag inside! We are doomed, doomed, doomed! I've lost Sharp Beak!"

"I told you we would get in trouble," Mary Beth said, tears welling up in her eyes.

"I'm sorry! I never should have had the idea!" I said, and I started crying.

"We are in a bit of a tickle, I mean pickle," Leo agreed.

"There you four are," came Astrid's voice. "I have been looking for you. You wait right here until I ask Mr. Itsasham to show Harold and me the new sleeping bags he is selling. The brand only allows certain establishments to carry its goods. Harold loves the brand."

"That I do," agreed Harold. He is around all the time now, which I didn't like at first, but his eyes look alive instead of dead like they used to.

Our hearts were racing and our stomachs churning as we watched Astrid and Harold walk into the store with Yabutiah and Mr. Pip. Jude the Dude and his camping club seemed to know about the new sleeping bags and invited themselves along.

After a million years had passed, everyone came out with smiles on their faces. Jude the Dude and his friends were happy because Harold had bought them all a new sleeping bag. I was so annoyed that, once again, Jude the Dude got something nice when he was so mean.

Astrid had Jasper's Cheep-Cheep bag in her hand, and Jasper started squealing. I stopped feeling annoyed and started to feel happy because my friends were no longer sad.

"You four look like you could use a Halloween movie," Astrid said, handing Jasper his bag. "Nova, you have my permission to take your friends into my sanctuary behind the front counter. You will find freshly popped popcorn, hot apple cider, and cozy blankets, including Birdie Blankie, waiting for you. But first, would you like to tell me what you four were doing in Mr. Itsasham's store?"

"I love Birdie Blankie! And my friends will love your sanctuary. But Astrid, if we go inside now, we won't be able to fill our bags with tons and tons of candy!"

"You needn't worry about bags overflowing with candy. Harold has taken care of that. Now, please tell me what you saw or heard. You are not in trouble, but I must know why you all look so concerned because I want to help you if I can."

I had the feeling Astrid already knew why we were in the store, so I decided I wouldn't repeat the scary things we heard. But Mary Beth told her everything.

"I see. Children, listen carefully. What you heard this evening was scary, and I won't pretend otherwise. However, I must ask you to temper your curiosity and stay away from secret conversations. Don't follow Miss Hypo unless you are walking into your classroom during school hours on a school day. Understand?"

"Miss Hypo is a bad, bad woman," Leo pointed out as he unwrapped another lollipop.

Astrid sighed, "This is much too heavy a burden for your young shoulders, no matter how strong you are. Let me carry the burden while you enjoy the rest of the evening, alright? I'll walk you over and start the movie myself."

"Can I kick Jude the Dude in the shins first? He's over at Not Your Grandma's Doily Yarn and Lace getting huge treats. He always gets everything he wants, no matter what he does! It's not fair!" I wanted to scream, but I didn't.

"Our friend, Drimwella Spindlewitt, might not be giving him the type of treat he is expecting. Besides, I advise you to resist the inclination to measure fairness, as you will find yourself on the losing end every single time," Astrid said.

"Not if I put Jude the Dude there first," I grumbled. Astrid pretended she didn't hear me. So, we followed Astrid, and she made us feel cozy and safe with her love.

Miss Hypo doesn't have love, which is why she is so mean and sad. Maybe I could try to love her. But I don't know how to love her when I don't like her, not one little bit. Maybe that's why love can be so hard.

Now, after Halloween, I have even more questions: Who is the old lady Miss Hypo was talking to? What is a compromise? Where is Miss Hypo's mother? What does education reform mean? What's The Cause? Why does the old lady think favors and compromises are worth more than money? Why do people love money so much? And why do horrible people get what they want when they don't follow the rules?

Chronicle the Fifth

Hiya, Everyone! It's me, Nova! Did you know that some people don't like whipped cream? Weird, right? Roland, Astrid's brother, is one of those people. Astrid told me not to say *those people* because it circumvents individuality.

She told me that, sometimes, when she goes to doctor appointments and tells them she is a florist by trade, they change how they talk to her because they start making assumptions about her intelligence based on her career, and not for the better. I thought everyone was friendly to Astrid because she's so pretty and intelligent, but I guess even pretty and smart people get treated with rudeness.

Being kind can be tricky, especially if your day is going super duper a million times terrible. My Thanksgiving started a super duper a million times terrible! First to start, the last day my mom was awake was on a Thanksgiving of yore.

The word yore means olden days. If you think about it, there are actually three more versions of the word your. Your, as in, I like your sweater. You're, as in, you are funny, and yer. Jasper's dad says yer regularly, as in "How yer doin'? I'll be informing Miss Hypo of my recent acquisition of knowledge next week. She'll be appreciative; I know it.

My mom loved Thanksgiving. We used to make turkey popcorn balls together. She would shape sticky caramel corn into balls, wrap the balls in Saran Wrap, and we would decorate them. Her turkeys would look so funny, with their legs, wings, faces, and tail feathers made of colorful construction paper.

When I finished mine, I would hold it up and say, "Mama, Mama! Look what I did!" She would get her Mama-love sparkle in her eyes, hug me, kiss me on the top of the head, and say, "My darling Nova. You did a wonderful job. I am so blessed to be your mama."

Then, I would say, "I am so blessed that you are my mama, and I will love you forever! When am I going to get a sister?"

Her shoulders would roll forward as she softly whispered, "That ship has sailed."

I told her that the ship should turn around and come back, but she only laughed and said that some boats never return to any harbor ever again. I think that means they crash or get eaten by a sea monster. So, since this year marks two years since her death, I woke up knowing it would be the third worst day of my life!

But Mr. Pip and me were hosting Thanksgiving dinner, and he needed my help to prepare for our guests, so I couldn't sit on my bed in my sadness all day like I wanted to. I wore my black leotard, black tutu, black leggings, black rainboots, and a black bow in my hair as a sign of mourning before stomping down the stairs. Stomping is an excellent way to let others know that you want attention but need space, and black is a good color to wear if you want others to see that you are sad, unless you always wear black, in which case you might need to work out an alternative.

Mr. Pip says there are healthier ways to communicate, but I don't know if I agree. When I peeked around the corner, I saw Mr. Pip leaning on the counter and reading the periodical from the day before. He was not looking in my direction, so I stomped even louder as I descended the last few steps.

Descended is the past tense of the word descend, which means to move downward.

"Nova! How happy I am to see you this morning. Can I get you something for breakfast?" Mr. Pip asked, setting down his periodical and smiling.

"Maybe some hot chocolate. It might cheer my downtrodden spirits," I said.

"Most certainly! Would you like to talk about the matters weighing on your heart?"

"No. I prefer to draw attention to myself while refusing to let anyone help me and then get upset that no one cared," I said, crossing my arms across my chest.

"If you are happy with your choice, I will not try to change your mind. Now, have a cinnamon roll with your hot chocolate, and let us prepare for dinner. The turkey will go in the oven in a couple of hours, and in the meantime, we have butterhorn rolls to bake. We made the chocolate cream pie and lemon raspberry pie yesterday, and we'll make the gravy when the turkey is done. Astrid is bringing ambrosia salad, stuffing, and an apple pie. Roland and Lottie are contributing sweet potato casserole and mashed potatoes. Beatrice mentioned green beans, cranberry sauce, and drinks. Are we forgetting anything?"

"No," I said with the biggest frowny face I could muster.

"Good. Do you want to set the table with the festive pumpkin napkins you chose? And the centerpiece you made with Astrid? I've never seen a cuter Thanksgiving hedgehog."

"I guess."

"Nova, I love you."

"Love you too."

Mr. Pip tried to cheer me up. He read me a story, colored Christmas pictures, and taught me how to roll dough. It worked a little because I laughed when I accidentally flung some dough onto Mr. Pip's framed photograph of his mother, which gave her a mustache. He said, "I've always been told that I look like my mother and never thought much of it. But now I see we are practically identical." Then, he started talking in a funny, old lady voice.

Our guests started arriving at 2:30 pm, beginning with Astrid and Beatrice. Astrid wore a burgundy dress covered in shiny, tiny brown maple leaves, and a thick copper sash was tied in a big bow behind her back. Her hat was a swirl of red, orange, and yellow leaves with pinecones and a copper bow. Of course, her earrings were shiny, tiny brown maple leaves, and her high-heel pumps were amber-colored. I asked her why she likes to get so fancy, and she said it helps her remember to have fun.

Every time I ask her, I get a different response, so I ask her repeatedly now. She once told me that dresses and heels remind her that she has a brain. She was a little grumpy that day.

Roland and Lottie, of course, were late. The only way Roland can be on time is by accident. They were smiling, giggling, and making silly jokes. Normally, I would have laughed, but I did not feel like laughing just then.

Finally, we all sat at the table, and I sat between Astrid and Roland. Mr. Pip blessed the food and thanked God for all the wonderful people in his life. And that's when I started to cry. Roland put his arm around me and didn't say a word. Astrid held my hand tight, and I could feel Beatrice smile. I wonder what she imagines I look like since she can no longer see with her eyes. Lottie blew me a kiss.

I hung my head and cried, "I just want my mama. I need my mama's love, hugs, and glittery mama eyes. It's hard for a child to be without a mama."

No one said anything because nothing needed to be said. Sometimes, when I sit in sadness and cry a good hard cry, all I want someone to do is sit with me for a while. My mama always told me it's okay to cry because crying cleanses the heart's wounds, and anyone who claims that crying is a sign of weakness is as wrong as someone who claims anger is a sign of power.

After a few minutes and many hugs, I felt better despite still feeling sad. I guess that happens sometimes. "Astrid, do you ever miss your dad?" I asked.

"Oh, Nova. I miss him every day, and I still cry now and then.

"You still cry?" I asked as I wiped the mucus and tears off my face with my sleeve.

"Of course I do. I love him, and while the memory of his loss brings tears, the memory of his love brings joy."

There was a long silence, and then Beatrice added, "You are mourning, my sweet child. We all know loss, and we all love you. While we cannot protect you from the realities of mortality, we can protect your light. Your mother expected us to give you at least that gift."

"You knew my mother?" I asked. "I thought Mr. Pip was the only one who knew my mother."

"Yes, we all knew your mother. She would visit Mr. Pip for a month every summer as a girl and a teenager. The last time we saw her, she was pregnant with you, wearing a long, flowing, cream-colored dress covered in soft gold sparkles, with a wreath made of ribbons on top of her formidable head of hair," Beatrice explained.

"Do I look like her?" I asked. Even though I know what my mother looks like, I like hearing what others think.

"You have her essence," Mr. Pip cut in. "Wild and magical, somewhere between a daisy floating on the wind and a star shooting across the heavens. You're, well, you're metaphoric momentum."

"Metaphoric momentum? I have never heard anything like that before in the whole wide world," I said.

"Yes, you, Nova, propel everyone around you forward because your boundless energy and curiosity are limitless. Without light, your momentum would come to an abrupt halt, which would end creativity and discovery. No one at this table can afford such a tremendous loss because you have stories to tell, songs to sing, murals to paint, and problems to solve."

When Mr. Pip said those kind words, I felt love grow bigger in my heart, and I made a note in my head to tell Jasper, Mary Beth, and Leo about their light; if I have it, so do they! Do you think they know they shine? Maybe our shininess reminds Miss Hypo of the light she had before her eyes turned dead-looking, and she is mad that we have what she lost. We'll need to hold a Best Friend Needs Assessment at our earliest convenience.

When people say, 'at your earliest convenience,' I think they mean 'as soon as you finish reading this email.'

"Did you make this lovely hedgehog centerpiece, Nova?" Lottie asked.

"Yes! I did! And I love her. Her name is Pear Prickle, and her favorite color is mermaid green; she only eats seaweed crackers because she is the only creature on earth who likes them, so she never has to share her food. She doesn't like mustard, the number nine, or people who pick their noses. I tried to introduce her to Birdie Blankie, but Birdie Blankie isn't ready to open her heart to anyone but me until next Tuesday."

Astrid giggled, gracefully picked up my plate, and piled on rolls, potatoes, and ambrosia salad. She knows that when a sad girl starts laughing, and the tears stop rolling, she is ready to eat again.

"Well, Nova, shall I tell you a story?" Mr. Pip asked.

"Yes! I love stories."

"What story do you want to hear?"

"I want to hear why you comb your bushy white mustache with a toy pony comb!"

"I would, too," Roland said, winking at Lottie. She giggled. They sure wink and giggle a lot. Is that what people do when they are in love?

"Very well. Here begins the explanation behind the mustache. When I was a young lad, not much taller than a very tall blade of the longest grass..."

I interrupted, "Technically, the longest blade of grass comes from a species of bamboo, and it..."

"Yes, yes, I know. The Dendrocalamus sinicus can grow to over 100 feet. I was there when Leo gave an ecology lecture on the interactions between living organisms. Brilliant child, he is. With respect to him, let me start again. When I was a young lad, not much taller than the counter in my mother's kitchen, I decided to grow a respectable mustache as soon as possible. You see, I had a rather wise, peculiar father with the best mustache in town."

"Your father was peculiar because he had a mustache?" Beatrice asked as she slowly ate a big spoonful of sweet potato casserole.

"No, no. He was peculiar – and he had the best mustache in town. If it had not been for his impressive facial hair, people might not have tolerated his obsessive conversations about cuckoo clocks. However, to him, the topic was out of necessity, as he was born near the Black Forest in Germany, the birthplace of the cuckoo clock.

During my father's lifetime, there was so much talk of WW2, the actual war, the atrocities committed, the devastation, the loss, and the sorrow, that cuckoo clocks were Dad's reminder of the resilience of goodness. You see, my father loved people and swore that the quickest way to lose a friend was to argue about matters of which neither party had absolute knowledge while insisting themselves both omniscient and omnipotent experts at every turn.

When he moved to the United States, he quickly learned to avoid questions about his life in Germany. As soon as he said 'German,' he was treated as if being born in the country made him their ambassador of policies and treaties, an expert on fashion trends, and an intimate friend of all of Europe and its secrets. Or, worse, responsible. So, to preserve his friendships and those of others, he talked about cuckoo clocks.

Fellow tiny mechanism enthusiasts could often be found at our dining room table, talking shop while Mother served shortbread cookies and cider. I liked hearing them laugh and frequently hovered around, trying to go unseen. During one of the gatherings, an angry neighbor came in, yelling profanities and threatening Dad. Mother told me to go to my room, but I didn't. I watched from around the kitchen counter. As a rough-and-tumble boy, I didn't want to miss witnessing a good fight, mainly because I knew my dad was stronger than any man there. One well-planted right hook to the jaw, and the screaming neighbor would be on his knees.

To my brief disappointment, my dad kept his fists to himself, said nothing, and remained sitting while this man kept hurling insults and accusations. Finally, the man paused, "Aren't you going to stand up and fight, or are you a coward just like your people?"

At those words, Dad stood up, and the room held its breath. Then, he offered his seat to the man who looked about ready to spit in his face. He said, "Please, rest. I can see you are hurting. I have seen pain and fear masked as anger many times in my life. It happens to me, too. Come now, have a seat. No one need do anything they will regret."

"What a rude neighbor!" Lottie exclaimed.

Mr. Pip continued, "Well, the neighbor sat down and cried. Dad put his hand on his shoulder without saying anything else. Mom brought him a sandwich. While he ate, the conversation returned to cuckoo clocks, and after half an hour, the neighbor cleared his throat and apologized for his outburst. He explained that his brother had been killed in the war, presumably by

Germans, and when he found out my father was born in Germany, years of grief snapped something in his brain, and he wanted someone to blame, someone to hurt.

My father forgave him on the spot, and the incident was never mentioned again. That day, Dad taught me what it meant to be a peacemaker. I promised myself I would be just like him, mustache and everything. A grown man using a tiny toy comb to tend to his facial hair hygiene does have a way of disarming contention. However, I must confess that at this point in my life, it has become a habit, nervous and otherwise."

"Wow!" I said.

"Wow is right," agreed Roland. "I hope to have such admirable self-restraint someday."

Mr. Pip sighed, "Me, too. I have made the mistake of avoiding and giving silent treatment to those who have offended me instead of using my words to resolve misunderstandings. I think such behavior can be as wounding as a punch to the face."

The best thing about a story like Mr. Pip's is that when it's over, people must sit and think about the implications for a while.

So, we sat, ate, and thought. "Mr. Pip? Do you know what I am thankful for?" I asked.

"Please, tell me," he answered.

"I am thankful for good people who make hard decisions, like not punching someone when they act like they need a good punching. Your dad protected your light that day because he knew you were watching. Good thing he did, too, or you might not be who you are today," I said.

"Out of the mouths of babes," Beatrice said.

All the adults smiled. I've heard people say that phrase before. What does it mean? I've also heard babies talk, and they don't make sense.

Also, why did I stop getting candy every time I used the bathroom? I've been potty-trained for nearly sixty-two months now, and I think that deserves an award of some sort. I am super duper a million times excited for Christmas! I have a bajillion Christmas movies to watch!

Then, me, Jasper, Mary Beth, and Leo are going to make Christmas cookies with Astrid. She promised to let us dip the spicy ginger cookies in chocolate and put the cranberry sauce in the thumbprint cookies. We'll see if she remembers her promise. As you know, Astrid is rather neat and tidy and gets a little stressed when the finished product gets messy. She says the creative process should be messy, not the finished product.

Maybe I will suggest putting messy cookies on one plate and perfect cookies on the other. I like sprinkles. And shiny things. And bright-colored bulbs. And lights. And happiness. And GIVING love because everyone deserves to feel loved.

Happy Thanksgiving!

Chronicle the Sixth

Hiya, Everyone! It's me, Nova! Merry Christmas! I'm a bit of a walking exclamation point this time of year; at least, Mr. Pip says so. He must have been the one who told Oswald the same thing. All the twinkling lights on the houses and the festive lawn decorations cause me to squeal, jump, and twirl! Some people decorate their homes with white lights, some with two colors, such as red and white, which is quite popular this year, while others use multi-colored, changing lights, or icicle designs, all in various sizes.

Mr. Pip told me he was too old to risk life and limb hanging lights from precarious architecture, so instead, he let me choose decorations for my room to make it as bright as I wanted. So, I did. I chose a small Christmas tree to place in the corner, wrapped in pink and purple tinsel and adorned with construction paper hearts, along with the ribbon scraps I have been collecting from Astrid's floral masterpieces.

Me and Jasper made a peacock for the top of the tree, and it looks rather swell. Leo said it looked like a Valentine's Day tree, and we should start over. Mary Beth said it wasn't quite her style, but she loved that I loved it.

I found two large containers in my drawer of craft supplies: one filled with green and red glitter, and the other with snowman confetti. And you know what I did? I took off the lids, held one container in each hand, tilted my head back, and twirled until they were empty.

When Mr. Pip walked by, I heard him whisper, "Well, at least she didn't cover the walls with glue first." He gives me a lot of good ideas when he whispers.

Our Christmas celebrations started with Astrid's annual one-woman rendition of Charles Dickens, *A Christmas Carol.* Per Roland, Astrid emphasizes a different passage every year. This year's choice was about the ghost of Scrooge's dead business partner, Jacob Marley, regretting his choice to care more about himself and his money than he did about others.

He was fettered and couldn't escape. Fettered means restrained with chains.

Jacob Marley could have released someone else from the temporary bonds of poverty and loneliness through love and kindness while he was alive, but he chose himself instead. Astrid quoted his words of regrets.

'Oh! Captive, bound, and double-ironed. . . not to know that any Christian spirit working kindly in its little sphere, whatever it may be, will find its mortal life too short for its vast means of usefulness! Not to know that no space of regret can make amends for one life's opportunities misused! Yet such was I! Oh, such was I! . . .At this time of the rolling year' . . . 'I suffer most. Why did I walk through crowds of fellow beings with my eyes turned down, and never raise them to that blessed Star which led the Wise Men to a poor abode? Were there no homes to which its light would have conducted *me*? . . . Mankind was my business, the common welfare was my business; charity, mercy, forbearance, and benevolence were, all, my business. The dealings of my trade were but a drop of water in the comprehensive ocean of my business!'

In the middle of her performance, I asked, "But, Astrid, I've heard you whisper while working on your floral arrangements that nothing is more lucrative than knowing business that isn't yours. So, if Jacob Marley's business was helping sad people, maybe you have the wrong kind of business. But you do a lot of thoughtful things for a lot of people, so maybe you get confused sometimes."

"Yes, as people, we often walk in contradictions. I'll explain it to you when you're older."

I don't know why she can't explain walking in contradictions now. I know I should be nice to everyone, but I still want to kick Jude the Dude in the shins when I see him. He knows it, too, and thinks it's funny to get on my nerves. But he also shares his lunch with a hungry-looking boy I only see in the lunchroom. Maybe Jude the Dude walks in contradictions, too.

Miss Hypo doesn't walk in contradictions because she is always the same meanness. So, when Astrid included her on our Christmas gift-giving list, I screamed! She told me to stop carrying on like one unhinged and suggested that me, Jasper, Leo, and Mary Beth all work together. So, today, I will tell you how we made Miss Hypo's gift, delivered it, and what happened afterward.

It all started at Astrid's house, of course, because she had the necessary accommodation for four seven-year-olds to make crafts and eat snacks until they burst into candy cane confetti a super duper million times over. Plus, since Mr. Pip's knee surgery, he has needed more naps at regular intervals, which seem to be getting closer together.

Astrid says he might be taking the same number of naps, but because I am home on Christmas break, I am noticing what has always been, which gives the illusion of more. She says the same thing happens when we start to notice goodness. The more we look for it, the more we see it in the most unexpected places from unexpected people. Goodness is one person sharing their heart with another.

"I don't want to share my heart with Miss Hypo," I said.

"Yeah! Have you seen what she does with hearts? She does this!" Jasper started pecking a pillow with his face.

"A dinosaur ate her heart," Leo stated matter-of-factly.

"I'd rather make a gift for someone else," Mary Beth added ever so politely.

"I am not asking you to put all your Christmas gifts in a bag on Christmas morning and drop them off at her door. I am asking you to make a small gift, which you will, at the very least, have fun making, if not fun giving. I've made five craft or treat examples, of which I expect you to choose two for Miss Hypo," said Astrid as she brought us to the kitchen to examine our choices.

There were two types of cookies: chocolate-dipped spicy ginger cookies and star-shaped sugar cookies with fancy frosting. There were also three ornaments: a popsicle stick Christmas tree, a wreath made from painted puzzle pieces, and a snowflake made out of blue and white buttons.

After much deliberation, me and my friends decided to share our hearts by making Christmas wreath ornaments and chocolate-dipped spicy ginger cookies. We chose the Christmas wreath because Leo wanted to know what sixteen liquid ounces of paint looked like when poured into a bowl, and the ginger cookies because Mary Beth said Miss Hypo hides chocolate in her desk drawer.

Do you know how you know if your hiding place isn't a very good one? If others know where it is.

Mary Beth and Jasper helped Astrid with the cookies while me and Leo worked on the wreaths. Then we switched. The cookies were hard because melted chocolate doesn't like to cooperate, but the wreaths were super duper a million times easy.

Here is what you do:

First, get a puzzle with a lot of pieces and lay them out so they are close together but not connected.

Second, paint all the puzzle pieces with thick green paint. Make sure it is Christmas green, not barf green. Let the paint dry.

Third, take a handful of pieces and make a circle; some will overlap. Once you like how your circle looks, glue it together with a hot glue gun.

Fourth, use red paint and make little dots all over your wreath.

Fifth, after the dots dry, apply a coat of clear-drying glue over the wreath and cover it with glitter according to preference. I used long white glitter that reminded me of sparkly snow. Leo said that since wreaths are often hung outside front doors, the roof protects the wreath from getting snowed on, so a snow-covered wreath is not an accurate representation of the snow and wreath relationship. I told him that his glitter-less wreath was not an accurate representation of the Christmas spirit. He shrugged.

Sixth, cut a piece of ribbon of your choosing, fold it in half, and hot glue the edges to the back of the wreath.

Ta-da! Now, you have an ornament to give away or keep. You can draw a picture to tape to the center of the wreath, like a butterfly, a cupcake, or a puppy. Leo drew a snake, and I drew a hippopotamus since the wreath is for Miss Hypo.

I don't know what Mary Beth chose, but you can guess what Jasper did.

Technically, you should ask an adult to help you with the hot glue steps, but I've been using hot glue since I was knee-high to a grasshopper. Leo said it's impossible to be knee-high to a grasshopper, and I would be less confusing to those around me if I simply said 'very young.' But that would be boring super duper a million times BORING! Astrid told me never to stop using the complexities of the English language, like hyperbole, alliteration, and metaphors, because that would be the equivalent of cutting off a peacock's feathers, burning them in a fire pit, and claiming you could still admire the now-destroyed plumage.

"We call ourselves advanced and yet applaud our efforts to obliterate the color and vibrancy of words that propel ideas and creativity – the very foundation of advancement. We talk of reading and writing as if they are heartless taskmasters, not the springboard for the full expression of the human condition that generations past could only dream of, as they were trapped in the fetters of illiteracy and ignorance. Let us not foolishly celebrate the impending death knell of the English language as one letter of the alphabet dances off the cliff of ignorance one at a time."

When Astrid paused to breathe, Leo raised his eyebrow and said, "Astrid, you don't make sense to me."

She laughed, so the rest of us laughed, too. Several hours and a gigantic mess later, Astrid helped us put the ornaments and cookies on a plate, wrap them in snowman-covered cellophane, and tie them with an enormous silver bow. Between the four kids, we tried five billion ways to avoid delivering Miss Hypo's gift.

"I can't go right now because my feet are too hot."

"I've already tried my best today, and my best won't be ready again for seven months."

"I have pockets."

"God didn't give us this world to be garbaged up. We need to take care of it. Let's pick up litter instead."

Astrid's last straw happened when Leo chased after her dog Crocus with two pencils, yelling, "I'm knitting a dog!"

"Children!' Astid said while smiling but looking a little bit ticked, "I will no longer tolerate your resistance. It was funny for a moment, but now all four of you must put your shoes upon your feet, don your coats, hats, and gloves, get into my car, and sing Christmas carols until the selfless generosity of the Christmas spirit descends upon us once more!"

We climbed into the car at her command and drove for a million minutes over a million miles to Miss Hypo's house. She lives in a gray townhouse that's squished between other townhouses. There were no Christmas lights without or within her abode, nor any hint of Christmas anywhere. No snowman on the doorstep, wreath on the door, or laughter-not even a ghost of laughter from Christmas past. I bet she has never laughed in her entire life!

I can always tell when a home is filled with laughter because it feels happy, even if the people inside are not laughing every second. Her neighbors, for example, had big green, red, and gold bulbs hanging on their shrubs, and the smell of freshly baked bread was coming from their door.

Miss Hypo's other neighbors had no exterior decorations, but I could hear the kids inside watching a Christmas movie and their mom saying, "Only one more handful of M&Ms, mister. I can see your other hand is quite full of candy, even if you are trying to hide it behind your back."

The mom had happiness in her voice, and I imagined a dark-haired little boy with brown eyes and a mischievous grin shoving both handfuls of candy in his mouth at once and pumping his cute, chubby legs as fast as he could toward the kitchen before his mom came and swooped him up, covering him with kisses.

The neighbor on the opposite side of the street was opening the door for her friends, and I wondered if she had ever tried to be Miss Hypo's friend. Nonetheless, it was our lot to approach this dark, unwelcoming, and cold house. Astrid knocked, and we all hid behind her.

After a couple of minutes, Leo rang the doorbell because he "just wanted to get this over with." There was still no answer. We all started to smile, thinking that we escaped Miss Hypo, but then her door cracked open.

"Oh great! This is the worst day of my life!" I probably should not have said that, but sometimes words zoom out of my mouth.

"Astrid," Miss Hypo said flatly.

"Crissy," Astrid said with a nod and a smile, indicating to Mary Beth to hand the cellophane-wrapped plate to our teacher. "Four of your students spent their entire afternoon making you a Christmas gift to brighten your day."

"Here, Miss Hypo. Merry Christmas!" Mary Beth said with her sweet smile. She almost always has a lovely smile, and I still haven't heard her scream when she gets stressed or frustrated. Miss Hypo stuck half her face out and snatched the plate from Mary Beth without uttering a word.

She was about to close the door until Astrid put her foot in the doorway. "Surely, Miss Hypo, you can take thirty-three seconds of your time and wrench yourself away from whatever pressing matters occupy your attention and at least muster the common courtesy to say thank you."

"Get your foot out of my doorway, or I will call the police and report you for trespassing," Miss Hypo hissed. I noticed her hair was wavy, her freckles were visible because she had no makeup on, and her eyes were brown instead of the blue contacts she usually wears. If she weren't so full of grumpiness, she would have looked pretty.

"Very well, Crissy. Shut your cold door to your cold house and listen to the icy beat of your cold heart. If you choose only yourself, in the end, you will only have yourself, and that is a torture no one should endure. Let yourself be loved, and if not loved, then liked, and if not liked, at least free from accusations of hatred toward the innocent," Astrid said.

"Good day, Miss Beeswax," Miss Hypo said with even more grumpiness! I wonder if someone's grumpiness can get so big that they become hateful without realizing what's happening.

"Good day and a Merry Christmas to you! Come along, children," Astrid said through a clenched jaw as she smoothed her dress and spun on her heel to face the opposite direction.

I was surprised that Miss Hypo didn't slam her door; instead, she gently closed it. We followed our fearless leader to the car like little ducklings, and I kept looking back at Miss Hypo's house. A light flickered on, and I saw her shadow watching us walk away, wiping something off her cheek. I will pretend it was a tear of remorse for her life choices.

As Astrid was about to close the car door and drive away, the neighbor from across the street rushed over in her slippers with a big, pale pink, fluffy blanket wrapped around her shoulders. She had beautiful, dark eyes and shiny, dark hair pulled up into a high, messy bun, and wore earrings shaped like red and white stockings.

"Excuse me, so sorry to interrupt. My name is Clara. I noticed you talking with Crissy, which probably makes me sound like some weird, nosy neighbor, but I'm super friendly and love people. Aside from when she moved in a few years ago, I've never seen her open the door for anyone. I bring her a present every year, and all I get is a set of brisk instructions to leave it on the doorstep and walk away. She keeps her car parked in her garage, so I never see her outside. Is she okay? Is she sick?"

Astrid paused and tilted her head toward Miss Hypo's house as if she could hear something the rest of us couldn't.

"Nice to meet you, Clara. I'm Astrid. I don't know Crissy well enough to know what goes on in her life, but I do know that she is a teacher, and these four children with me are her students."

"She's a teacher?! How fun. Maybe I will give her a gift card for school supplies this year. My sister is also an elementary school teacher, and I know they work on a tight budget." She paused, then shook her head and knelt to greet us. "Hi, kids! It's my pleasure to meet you. I'm Clara. If you wait here, I will grab you a Christmas goodie bag. My friends and I are making a bunch to bring to the Senior Center tomorrow, and we have extras. Would you like that?"

"Yes, please!" We said in unison.

"Wonderful. Is that okay, Astrid? I should have asked you first."

"Of course! These four worked hard today and could use some kindness in return."

While Clara ran across the street, Astrid kept her head tilted toward Miss Hypo's house and hummed softly. She laughed for no reason, rolled her eyes, and then put her palm on her forehead. I didn't ask any questions, though, because Astrid is unique, like me! Unique people do unique things. Instead, I smiled at her and hugged her. She hugged me back. I love hugs!

Sure enough, Clara came running over with five Christmas goodie bags nearly the size of grocery bags! The bags were green with a golden shimmer, and they were also quite heavy.

"Goodness! Thank you so much!" Astrid said, and we all nodded in agreement as Clara handed us the bags one by one.

Mary Beth pulled a Christmas wreath ornament from her pocket and gave it to Clara. In the middle, she had drawn a picture of a teddy bear.

"This is for you, Clara. I knew we might meet someone special tonight, so I made an extra ornament."

"You made this?" Clara was impressed.

"We all made ornaments today for Miss Hypo, and cookies. But she didn't like them," Mary Beth said. Mary Beth almost started to cry, and I wanted to kick Miss Hypo in the shins for making my friend cry.

"I think I know why Crissy opened her door," Clara said, winking at Astrid. "You know who would love your ornaments?"

"Who?!"

"The people at the Senior Center. I bet we could arrange a time for your jolly group to come over and deliver the ornaments individually. You would brighten their whole month! What do you think?"

The four of us jumped up and down and squealed, "Please, please, please!!!"

Astrid smiled one of her happiest smiles and said, "Of course. Perhaps Clara and I can exchange numbers and make the arrangements?"

"Wonderful! I love Christmas!" Clara said.

"I'll text you my personal and work phone as I am often at work," Astrid said as her thumbs started flying around on her phone.

As soon as Astrid sent the numbers, Clara began saving them in her contacts. "I think I already have your work number for some reason. Do you work at The Bee's Knees across town?"

"I do indeed."

"She doesn't just work there; she owns it!" I interrupted, almost shouting.

"I love your floral shop, or at least the flowers I get from there, as I have never been myself. I have an aunt with the last name of Duncecap, and she occasionally brings me bouquets for my birthday or Valentine's Day. Have you met her?"
"Yes! I knew her very well. We've had many a conversation and debate, and my job would not be nearly so rewarding without her," Astrid said.

"Can I hug you? Anyone who tries to understand my aunt deserves a hug. She has no idea how rude she can be," Clara said.

"Yes, I suppose so." Astrid is one of the most uncomfortable huggers I have ever seen in my entire life! She's good at hugging kids but gets stiff and awkward when hugging one of her peers. I'll need to talk to her about that later. Hugs are supposed to be bendable and soft, freely given and freely received, as she would say.

I don't know how many wreath ornaments we made, but we delivered them all individually. Our feet were super duper a million times tired at the end!

We met many interesting people and I asked them lots of questions, because, as you know, you can learn anything if you ask lots of questions! I noticed that some people ask a question that isn't the one they actually have. Why?

Chronicle the Seventh

Hiya, Everyone! It's me, Nova! Did you know that when we humans were made, we were supposed to have tear ducks instead of tear ducts? So, the next time you see someone crying, pretend their tears are little ducklings running around on their face.

Jasper told me, Leo, and Mary Beth that his dad had told him about tear ducks when he was crying just a few days ago. As soon as he imagined fluffy yellow bird babies playing up and down his cheeks, he started laughing. But Leo quickly pointed out that ducklings are not potty trained, so if they run around on your face, you run a significant risk of stinky brown spots.

School makes my tear ducks tired because it has not been easy lately. Miss Hypo has even more grumpiness than before, and Jude the Dude came back from Christmas break with an extra angry spark in his eyes. Some people have sparkles, which means they are kind. But sparks are a sign of danger.

Well, me and Jude the Dude got in a fight because he was making fun of Leo during class. I told him to stop, and then he pulled my hair and told me my brain was as bouncy as my curls, and bounced brains are as useful as bounced eggs, broken and worthless.

I got super duper a million times mad and, like any reasonable seven-year-old would, kicked him in the shins as hard as I could with my bright pink high-top sneakers decorated with rhinestones in a swirly pattern I made myself. Jude the Dude made a horrible sound, and the class turned to look at us. He fell to the floor and grabbed his shin as if I'd broken his leg, wailing and writhing. For a second, I was worried that I had broken his leg, and I felt terrible. Then, I saw him wink at me when Miss Hypo came clomping around the corner in her high heels, and I almost kicked him again.

"Nova Flaherty! You, young lady, are to march straight to the principal's office, where you will be disciplined and sent home immediately," Miss Hypo yelled, standing over me and repeatedly pointing at the door as if she were an airplane traffic controller. "We do not tolerate violence in this school, and I will not tolerate such a selfish and wild girl in my classroom. We are kind, inclusive, and patient, and you can expect to be assigned to the other second-grade teacher, who might find you less infuriating than I do. Now get out!"

I didn't bother protesting because kicking Jude the Dude was wrong, even though he pulled my hair and hurt my sensitive scalp. But I did wink at Leo before marching out of the classroom with my head held high. By the time I got to the office, I was crying so hard I was nearly choking on my sobs. I tried to imagine tiny ducklings running around my cheeks to stop myself from shedding so many tears, but I only cried harder because I knew Astrid, who always picks me up from school, would be disappointed.

The principal's door was open when Astrid arrived, and she breezed in as if they were expecting her. Her dress was made of white eyelet fabric, tied with a thick, icicle blue sash, and a matching half hat and t-strap pumps with silver bow-shaped stud earrings. I wanted to tell her that she reminded me of an Easter basket, but she only had time to kiss me on the head.

She talked to the principal forever, and I sat in the Shame Chair forever. Astrid says the chair for kids sent to the front office is named the Shame Chair because it's intended to let everyone know that a child is guilty of making a mistake.

When she finally emerged, her emerald green eyes were red around the edges, and I hung my head. She hugged me, took my hand, and told me we were going home for the day. Like I said, I knew Astrid was disappointed with me, but the good thing about

Astrid is that she always lets me explain what happened before she talks.

"Astrid," I began as I climbed into the backseat of her Serene blue PT Cruiser, "I kicked Jude the Dude in the shins super duper a million times hard, and he will definitely have a bruise on his leg in the morning. I know I made the wrong choice, but he was making fun of Leo, and when I tried to defend Leo, he pulled my hair and told me that I had a bounced and broken egg brain. Just saying Jude the Dude's name makes me hoppin' mad! And the worst part about kicking him was that my favorite rhinestone fell off my shoe. Do you think it will be there tomorrow?"

"I don't know about the rhinestone, but I know you won't be at school tomorrow or the rest of the week."

"What? That's not fair! Does Jude the Dude get to go to school? I bet he does. Why am I always, always, always the one who gets in trouble?" I started crying all over again.

"Nova, the decision is fair. Jude was rude, but his behavior does not excuse your behavior," Astrid explained.

"I guess you are about to tell me that I should go find an adult next time. Do you want to know what happens when I go find an adult? I still get in trouble because no one listens to me, and when no one listens to me, I want to scream, and when I scream, I get sent out of the classroom. Jude the Rude Dude has never been sent to the principal's office, and he never will! It's not fair!"

Astrid glanced back at me through the rearview mirror, and I could see love in her eyes. "You getting sent home for kicking Jude is fair, but Jude getting away with pulling hair and making fun of others is not fair. So, you are correct in that sense. I call what you are experiencing infuriating unfairness, which means the unfairness is so blatant and preventable that anger bubbles up inside you until you explode like a volcano. Does that sound about right?"

I had to think about her question for a few seconds because sometimes I feel like a volcano for no reason. "Yes," I finally said. "An exploding volcano sounds right. What am I supposed to do when I feel like that?"

"There are many ways to manage those feelings. Some people use exercise, others meditate or create art. Some do all three and everything in between. I still haven't mastered my own emotions, so be patient with yourself. In the meantime, you will spend the rest of the week working on a project that can bring your classmates happiness, including Jude."

"What?! Why? Can't I bring everyone else happiness and leave him out? That's what he would try to do to me. I know he would."

"Once again, Nova, how someone treats you is not a litmus test for how you treat them. I'm not suggesting you make him a plate of cookies or put a Friend of the Year banner over his desk. Rather, I suggest you show kindness to all your classmates, including him. Besides, Miss Hypo has agreed to let you remain in her classroom if you can apologize through an act of service."

"What if I don't want to stay in her classroom?" I asked, frowning my biggest frown ever.

"Do you want to be in the same class as Jasper, Leo, and Mary Beth?"

"You know I do, Astrid."

"So, if you want to be in the same class as your friends, you must stay in Miss Hypo's class."

I crossed my arms and squeezed them against my chest, fighting with myself. I knew if I apologized, I would get to stay with my friends, but I also knew that if I apologized, Jude the Dude would win again.

"Don't let Jude be the variable that sways your decision," Astrid said as if she were reading my mind. "Instead, focus on your friends and bring a little sunshine into the lives of others. What do you think would bring sunshine to your classmates?"

"A piñata. Piñatas are bright and happy and filled with candy. Can you teach me how to make a piñata?" I asked.

"I can, but do you know that I know an expert piñata maker?"

"You do? Who? Tell me, tell me, tell me?" My seatbelt could hardly restrain me because I was jumping around in my seat so hard.

"His name is Charles Pip!"

"What?! Mr. Pip is an expert piñata maker and didn't tell me? Yay! He can help me! This is the best day of my liiiife!"

***

Astrid and Mr. Pip talked in hushed tones when she dropped me off at his house. When someone talks in hushed tones, they whisper about important things they don't want the people nearby to hear. When they were done, Mr. Pip started combing his bushy white mustache with a teal toy pony comb and went to his room to think or take a nap.

When he came out a million years later, he asked me what I had been learning at school. I stared at him until I finished chewing my vanilla and lemonade cupcake. Technically speaking, he knew I kicked Jude, but he didn't know what I was learning, and maybe the question was his way of starting a conversation. Still, I do not like adults asking questions that they already know the answer to. But I decided not to make an issue out of his infraction.

Infraction means a violation of a law or agreement.

"I do all my book learning with Astrid. In Miss Hypo's class, I fill out worksheets. They are super duper a million times boring. She took away art time because she hasn't any imagination; she doesn't even like colors or happiness. Technically, she said she took it away because the school doesn't have money for supplies, but the kids in other classrooms still have art time. I wonder if she forgot that kids have eyes and ears."

"I am sorry to hear such a sad report. Have you truly learned nothing from Miss Hypo? I know she can be a difficult woman, but she is intelligent and must have something to teach you," Mr. Pip said. His tone sounded like he knew what she could teach me if she wanted.

"I thought you were talking about school smartness, like science and math. Miss Hypo has not taught me anything that Astrid has not already taught me. But she has taught me lots of other things. For example, she has taught me that if a student wants to be happy in her class, they must ask no questions and be easily distracted by a computer screen. The screens are better at keeping kids out of teacher's hairs than anything else. Why do teachers want to keep kids out of their hairs? Are there a lot of kids trying to get in? Do you know what else? When I know something will get in my hairs, I just stay away from it. Lollipops can get in my hairs, but I make an exception because they are so delicious.

Did you know that a famous candy store holds the world record for the biggest lollipop? They do, and it weighed 7,000 pounds. I wonder how many bags of sugar were required? And who ate it? Do you think they broke it into big pieces and sold it? Maybe some old person put their chunk of lollipop in a jar and will use it as a conversation starter when they run out of things to talk about with their grandchildren. And how could they prove it came from that particular lollipop? Maybe a different candy company tried to do the same thing, but theirs weighed 6,789 pounds, and the broken pieces were the same size. Who would know? Would they give a certificate of verification? And how would they prove the signature was from the right person?”

Mr. Pip sighed. “To answer your first question, some teachers are wonderful and irreplaceable because they love and inspire their students. However, some teachers don’t love the children they teach, so they consider any interruption by the child an irritation that could be remedied if the child were less childlike.

They want children to do what they tell them to do without causing any interruption, irritation, or requisite unplanned time away from their carefully laid plans.”

“Children are fun and happy. Being adultlike is the problem because it means you are super duper a million times grumpy and complaining about the cold and carbs. What are carbs? Are they diseases that make you fat?”

“Carbohydrates are nutrients that give our bodies the energy to move and think. They are not a disease,” Mr. Pip explained.

“Do you know what else? People litter, and God did not make this world for it to be garbaged up. I’ve already told Astrid.”

Mr. Pip started laughing.

“Don’t laugh at me!” I really hate when people laugh at me.

“I am not laughing at you. I am laughing because you bring me joy. First, we talked about lollipops, then carbohydrates, and now we are on to the plague of litter. How your mind operates is unique, fast, and intelligent; you bring joy to my heart.”

“But, Mr. Pip! Jude the Dude always laughs at me! Does he get to be joyful while making me sad? He gets to be mean until I kick him, and I am the one who gets punished while he goes on making fun of whoever he wants!” I exclaimed.

“Oh, goodness, no. The laughter of which I speak comes from the delight of living, not at the expense of another. Making fun of others or trying to intentionally upset them for your own entertainment is neither funny nor kind. As you grow, you'll find that those who use people rather than value them are some of the loneliest and saddest you will ever meet. I should think that Jude is not as happy as he pretends."

"What does value mean?" I asked.

"To value a person means to appreciate and love them," Mr. Pip said.

"Oh. If a person doesn't love at least one other person besides themselves, then they are sad and lonely?"

"Correct, even when surrounded by people," Mr. Pip answered while nodding his head.

"If I am sad, does that mean I do not love people?"

Mr. Pip hugged me and patted my hair, "No, no, no. Not at all. Nova, you are one of the most effusively loving seven-year-olds I have ever met because you shower everyone with affection and joy wherever you go. Still, we all have days when we feel gloomy and down, and that's a normal part of life. However, withholding good when it is within your power to give it consumes the soft parts of your heart. What is the opposite of soft?"

"Hard! You're going to ask me if carrying a hard heart in my chest would make me happy, and of course, it would not!"

"Remember that we choose whether our hearts will be soft or hard. No one can decide for you. Should we make the piñata to keep our hearts soft and add happiness to the world?"

"We're not adding happiness to the world. We're only adding it to my second-grade class!"

"One by one, Nova. World peace and happiness will only happen one by one. To make a piñata, we will need the following materials: cardboard, a balloon, old periodicals, flour, water, twine, colorful tissue paper, candy, scissors, and tape. Why don't you find those things while I sit down and rest for a moment?"

"Yay! Yay! Yay! I will search right away!" I ran upstairs to my art closet to collect the supplies, and by the time I came back downstairs, Mr. Pip had already fallen asleep. I placed two cookies on his favorite plate, made of porcelain and decorated with delicate pink roses, and set it next to his recliner. The plate used to belong to his mom. When he talks about his mom, he smiles and laughs. She must have been a delight.

Then I heard a noise and knew Jasper had arrived. Of course, Jasper doesn't knock; he squawks and runs into the door with his head.

"Hiya, Jasper! I was hoping you would come over today because school was absolutely terrible. Is Leo okay? Do you want to help me make a piñata? I need to make one for our class before I can return to school. I'm supposed to show kindness as an apology for kicking, you know who," I explained with the utmost seriousness.

"You're making a piñata?"

"Yes, I'm in the process anyway and just gathered the supplies from upstairs."

"What is the piñata going to look like?" Jasper asked. Right then, I knew that I could say two words to make Jasper feel loved and happy for the rest of the day: "A chicken."

"Ba-cluck! Ba-cluck!" Jasper pretended to scratch and peck as I showed him the tissue paper. He has a particular fondness for paper for some reason.

A few minutes later, Leo and Mary Beth joined us. "Thanks for standing up for me," Leo said. "You don't need to get yourself in trouble next time because I ignore Jude the Dude. Listening to the mean words of a mean person is pointless. Plus, I'm stronger than him anyway."

Mary Beth added, "We are lucky to have a friend with a big heart who cares very much."

"And I'm lucky to have friends who come visit me even though I've been kicked out of school for four days," I declared, slapping my hand on the counter.

"Ba-cluck! Ba-cluck," Jasper said again before pausing, "I can't believe I am making all this noise, and Mr. Pip is still asleep."

"I am awake, my dear children," said Mr. Pip from his chair.

"You are not lucky; you are blessed."

PRINCIPLE

Chronicle the Eighth

Hiya, Everyone! It's me, Nova! Guess what? Me and Jasper, and Leo, and Mary Beth got to go with Astrid to a fancy party. She heard us lamenting the lack of a school Valentine's party and asked if we wanted to help her with Doily Dayle's Valentine's party, A Tale of Two Hearts.

Lament means to express sorrow, which is different than complaining when you don't want to do the dishes. Mr. Pip calls that complaining, whining. There are certainly a lot of words to describe the same thing. Leo thinks everyone would understand each other better without so many word options.

I told Astrid what Leo said, and she said that her soul would be forever sorrowful if her vocabulary were limited to the remaining ashes left smoldering at the cremation of the English language. Leo pointed out that her soul might not be sorrowful if she had never known that other words were a possibility, and she said that our souls always yearn for much more than we can ever understand.

I guess Astrid and Leo just like different things. Mr. Pip says that different perspectives and opinions are necessary for progress, and if everyone thought and did the same thing, the world would be "a most nap-inducing place indeed."

After waiting and waiting and waiting, the day of the party finally arrived! My friends got dropped off early at The Bee's Knees because Astrid expects punctuality. She says that to be late to an agreed-upon appointment is an act of rudeness because you waste the precious time of the person waiting. I don't ever, ever, ever need to worry about punctuality because, on party days, I wake up at 5:15 AM and start knocking on Astrid's door by 5:22 AM. If you're wondering how I get dressed so fast, it's because I go to bed in my next-day outfit to save time.

I know more about Astrid than anyone else because I don't mind my own business. I can't! Other people are way too interesting! Don't tell anybody, but I think Astrid's time obsession reached unhealthy levels when she was seven years old. But that's another story. Back to the happenings at The Bee's Knees.

Almost anyone could have smelled the roses when the doors of the floral shop opened unless their nose got bitten off by a werewolf or a badger or a wolverine or a ferocious fox. Oh, what about a fabulously fancy, ferocious fox? I enjoy practicing alliteration by seeing how many words I can string together that start with the same sound. Do you like the smell of roses? I do, but I do not like when old ladies wear rose perfume because, first of all, it doesn't smell like roses, and second of all, it smells like the takes-itself-too-seriously cheap soap found at expensive hotels, and third of all, it gives me a headache. And I do not appreciate headaches. They give me grumpiness!

Red, white, purple, and pink roses covered every imaginable surface. I've seen Astrid's floral shop filled up for other big events, but this was super duper a million times more than any of those! There were huge arrangements and tiny bouquets, some tied with thick white satin ribbon and some with gold. Long-stemmed versions filled delicate glass vases, and Astrid looked like a beautiful Valentine herself! She wore a rose-pink dress with white tulle under the skirt and tiny white pearls around the waist, and I wondered if there would be a heart for her heart at A Tale of Two Hearts.

"Hello, Nova, Leo, Jasper, and Mary Beth," Astrid said, interrupting my thoughts. "I am ever so grateful for your willingness to help with A Tale of Two Hearts. As you can see, we have an abundance of flowers for the party, but never an excess. One cannot possibly have an excess of flowers."

"Where will the party be, Miss Astrid?" asked Mary Beth.

"The party is being held at Braggart Estates in their exquisite ballroom. Harold has even arranged for a string quartet to play romantic music," Astrid answered.

"Romance? YUCK!" Jasper yelled before falling to the ground.

"Yes, romance, when two hearts yearn to become one."

"Do you like yucky romance?" I asked.

Astrid looked down at her hands, scraping the edge of her cuticles with her fingernail, and said, "I believe in romance that transcends atmospheres, events, and attire. The only romance worth having is the romance that leads to love, true love."

"What's the difference between love and true love?" Leo wanted to know.

"True love is an earnest desire for the well-being of another; to shower them with affection and attention, to seek ways to lighten their burden, to laugh, and to say sorry. Love, as a passing word between two people, easily ends when the complexities of life enter the scene," Astrid explained.

"Have you ever been in love, Astrid?" Mary Beth asked. Astrid blushed and looked toward the ceiling, and I could tell she was watching her words float out of her brain. Do your words ever float out of your brain? Mine don't. They get in a word jam, which is sort of like a traffic jam, and then they shove their way out and zoom around, usually crashing into someone else and causing a ruckus.

Did you know that when you are legally allowed to drive a car and do so, you are required to pay for insurance? I once heard Mr. Pip say that one could spend a year's salary on insurance, go bankrupt in the process, and still incur thousands of dollars in medical bills. I think Mr. Pip was exaggerating when he said thousands of dollars. Do you know how much money that is? Mr. Pip has a locked safe with thousands of dollars inside (I know this because I was spying on him when he thought I was asleep), and there is no way a doctor would ask anyone to pay such a high price. Doctors are supposed to be nice, and it is not nice to take away people's life savings.

"I love sharks, snakes, and dinosaurs," Leo said.

Astrid smiled again and walked toward her sanctuary, "We can save the discussion of love and romance for another time because right now, I must present your formal clothing inspired by the love-obsessed holiday."

"Can I get something else instead?" Leo asked as Astrid brought clothes hanging from hangers and covered in bags.

"You have yet to see what I chose for you, so how can you object already?" Astrid asked with a wink.

"I already know I won't like it because I don't like clothes that stop my arms and knees from bending. They make my body scream. I hate clothes with buttons, collars, long sleeves, and long legs. I like basketball shorts and T-shirts," Leo said.

"I must regretfully inform you of the non-existent nature of formal basketball shorts and T-shirts, so I am afraid you must make do. And I might remind you that the only appropriate response to a person presenting you with a gift is 'thank you.'"

"But if I am not thankful for the gift, why do I need to thank you? It doesn't make any sense," Leo said.

"You say thank you because the gift giver chose to think of you and do something kind. Be grateful for the thoughtfulness, even if the gift is not what you wanted."

I don't know what Leo said after that because I screamed with happiness when Astrid uncovered the dress she chose for me. It was made of royal purple tulle, with puffy sleeves, a twirly skirt, and a thick white sash. The hem had probably been dipped in glitter and then turned upside down to let the extra sparkles fall like raindrops on the rest of the dress. Astrid made a white bow to go in my hair; I could tell because a tiny rhinestone bumblebee was in the middle. I don't have my ears pierced, so I got to wear pink heart-shaped clip-on earrings.

Mary Beth's dress was ballet pink without glitter, but she still thought it was beautiful because it had long sleeves, a flowy skirt, black buttons down the back, and a black sash with a rhinestone bumblebee in the middle—just like my hairbow! She had a black headband, too, and because she had pierced ears, she got to wear dainty pearls.

The good thing about liking three colors like Mary Beth does is that no one needs to guess what to give you. On the other hand, if you want every color, like me, it also makes giving easy. Either way, people are different.

Jasper and Leo? Way, way different. Jasper likes vests, so Astrid chose black slacks, a long-sleeved red collared shirt, and a white vest covered in tiny red cardinals to honor his favorite bird. A black bow tie with a rhinestone bumblebee made him look really swell! Jasper loves vests and bow ties because he says they are 'strong man clothes.' I wonder how many vest- and bow-tie-wearing strong men are in his life.

Leo's outfit was simple. Black pants, a long-sleeved white collared shirt, and a red kerchief folded in the front pocket. The kerchief was embroidered with snakes, and one had a rhinestone bumblebee as an eyeball!

"The snakes are not realistic. A snake would never be born with a bumblebee for an eye," he said upon inspection.

Astrid smiled. She sure was smiling a lot that day! Once we were all dressed up in our fancy new duds, we drove to Braggart Estates. None of us had ever seen a house so huge in real life!

Leo said it might be a house, but it wasn't a home because too many lights were turned off.

Before leaving the car, Astrid turned to face the back seat, "Come, come, children. You must be made aware of a matter of the utmost importance. Attendees, the people attending the party, will be wearing their finest apparel and possess a complete disdain for messes, loud and unexpected sounds, and candy."

"I knew if we came to a party for adults that the first rule would be No Fun! I bet they don't like carbs, either. Mr. Pip told me all about carbs," I said, folding my arms and slumping back into my seat.

I find that slumping is the best way to clearly communicate annoying disappointment.

"Nova, Nova, dear. I am teasing, at least about the candy. Fine chocolate in various shapes and wrappers will be everywhere, and I kindly ask that you four not overindulge. You'll receive your bag of chocolate confections upon our return to The Bee's Knees. Aside from abstaining from overindulging in chocolate, please help set up the flowers, plates, goblets, silverware, and conversation starter cards at each table and bring the dishes to the kitchen when the guests are done eating."

"Are we helping because real servers are too expensive?" Mary Beth asked.

"Servers are not too expensive, at least not for Harold. He asked specifically for the four of you to help under my supervision. We will set up most of what I listed in advance, but the conversation starter cards are wrapped in silk and placed in a fine box to be delivered, with one set of cards at each table while the guests await their food. I find people to be less guarded about their opinions, with hunger at the forefront of their minds. Do my instructions make sense?"

"Why are the cards wrapped?" Mary Beth asked.

"Excellent question. The cards are wrapped because presentation is everything at parties like this, from the people to the food to simple conversation cards. Appeal to the eye, and so much gets overlooked. Rather ironic," Astrid said.

"Is that why you dressed us up like a Valentine?" Leo asked.

"Perhaps, or perhaps I simply thought you would look cute."

"I am not cute. I am a dinosaur," Leo assumed his velociraptor pose, and I knew he would be in the Jurassic World Imagination Station for the rest of the party.

"Even velociraptors can don a nice outfit every once in a while," Astrid said in a motherly tone.

"No, they can't. They're dinosaurs, and dinosaurs don't wear clothes," Leo said.

"Well, certainly refrain from running around nude!" Astrid said, putting her hand on her hip. "I never before supposed I would discuss the validity of dinosaur clothing with an incredibly intelligent seven-year-old. Delightful. Now, onward we go."

We followed behind her like four waddling ducklings, except we weren't waddling, and we didn't have bills. Or feathers. Mostly, we were like ducklings because we were walking in a single-file line.

Inside, the ballroom was humongous, with lots of wood and unique carved details everywhere. The paintings on the wall were super duper a million times boring, mostly of odd, grumpy shapes and grumpy-looking people with crinkly skin and serious faces that probably never smiled once in their entire lives.

Why do people choose odd-shaped grumpiness as their home décor? Astrid said that most people like what they are told to like by the hidden rules within their society. If all these rules keep being enforced, me and my friends are doomed, doomed, doomed to boringness for the rest of our lives!

The orchestra was playing the romantic music Astrid had promised, and I wanted to go to sleep! Mary Beth twirled, spun, and leaped across the floor. She is as graceful as a gazelle. When I told her my observations regarding sameness and boringness, she said, "My grandmother always told me that if you're the one who sees a problem no one else sees, you're the solution. Here comes Harold now; tell him."

She was right. Harold walked down the big flight of stairs wearing shiny black shoes and a black suit with a black bow tie. Even his tie had a rhinestone bumblebee in the middle! I wonder if other attendees will be wearing one, too. He also has bright, white teeth. His smile and eyes used to be mismatched like I've told you before; one looked happy, and the other looked empty. But something happened, and now they match with happiness! I bet he would wear a Valentine's tie if Astrid asked him to because he has romantic feelings for Astrid, but he is not the colorful, clothes-wearing type, so she would never ask. Trust me.

I took a deep breath, put on my courage, grabbed Mary Beth's arm, and marched right over to him before he got too involved in a conversation with Astrid or, worse, touched her arm. It's gross when adults who like each other touch hands or hug. You should only hug your friends. "Hiya, Harold! This is a swell sort of place you have here. But I have some sad news. Your party décor is afflicted with sameness and needs a little more excitement, or all the attendees will start taking out their phones and tapping their thumbs on their screens as if the phone could prevent the present and predict the future! (I heard Astrid describe a phone like that a few times) Think about it! Why bother dressing up and being polite about eating treats when you could stay at home, wear comfortable clothing, and eat as many treats as you want if you're going to stare at your phone for hours anyway?"

"I couldn't agree more, Nova. What do you have in mind?" Harold asked, putting his hand on his hip just like I had my hand on my hip.

"You agree with me?" I asked.

"Most wholeheartedly, yes! In fact, I was planning on your observation, and I trust the rest of your friends feel the same?"

Mary Beth twirled and curtsied, saying, "Yes, sir."

The velociraptor and the chicken were only a few feet away and nodded their assent. Assent means agreement.

"From what Astrid tells me, I know the four of you are quite creative. I'll give you a few minutes to discuss ideas, and then I am sure we can find supplies for whatever you need somewhere in this enormous house," Harold laughed and winked at us, then turned to Astrid and touched her elbow! Yuck!

"What do you guys think we should do?" Mary Beth asked. "I wonder what is written on the conversation cards? My parents love to discuss news, politics, and the impending end of the world. So, I bet the party attendees will discuss the same subjects."

 "Adults end up talking about that stuff no matter what they start talking about," Leo added.

"We could draw pictures they could color, like at restaurants," Jasper said.

"Yes! We could give each person four crayons, but the good kind of crayons, not the waxy kind that gets all sticky and smeary," Mary Beth said. "I don't like sticky, muddy, slimy, gooey, or other gross textures." She is so prim and proper. I would probably implode if I had to be prim and proper like her.

"Guys!" I whisper-shouted. "Do you remember the conversation we overheard on Halloween? The one between Miss Hypo and the old lady who said she makes deals with people who pay in favors and compromises? And The Cause?"

"Scary, scary, scary!" Jasper said.

"Don't you want to know what they were talking about?" I asked.

"Astrid told us to temper our curiosity and stay away from secret conversations, remember?" Leo asked. "Those were her exact words. We should do what she says."

"I didn't say anything about listening to secret conversations. We should replace the questions in the conversation starter cards with ones about The Cause. We'll be able to tell who is a member of the secret society, and who is not just by the looks on their faces!"

"How are we going to explain ourselves to Astrid and Harold? They'll figure out it was us," Mary Beth pointed out.

"Could we ask the question in a way that sounds different but asks the same thing? Adults do it all the time," I said.

"Astrid will figure us out anyway. She's too smart," Leo said.

Just then, Astrid walked up behind us. Usually, I would hear the clickety-clack of her shoes, but this time, it startled me!

"I thought you four might want to look at the questions inside the conversation starter card boxes for fun. You can untie the bow on this one," she gave us a wink, smoothed her dress, spun on her heel, and walked toward the front door. We opened the box carefully and read the cards.

Some of the questions were: Have you ever had to choose between comfort and conviction? Do you prefer old ways or new opportunities? If the world turned upside down, which way would you walk? How many surgeries have you had? When was the last time you were physically capable of running? Are you an outside or out-of-doors person? In what way would you change the lives of the people of Doily Dayle for the better?

Leo stared blankly, "They should talk about science instead. Science is interesting and so simple. Why does everything have to mean something in a conversation? Why can't things just be?"

"I don't know. Maybe we should forget about rewriting the questions on the cards. Instead, let's ask Harold if he has silly string, glitter, and streamers. All exciting parties have those three things," I said.

As Harold had promised, he gave us all we requested. "Whatever you do with these is your business. I don't want any details," he said.

Soon, the guests started to arrive. I had seen many of them before: Millie Rumourus, Marge and Madge, Mrs. Duncecap, Mr. Pip, and Oswald, of course.

I was super duper a million times vexed and surprised when Miss Hypo walked in with a man who had hair as red and almost as big as mine! And he had five muddy and stinky brown dogs with him! He was younger than Astrid and way, way younger than Miss Hypo, rather thin, freckled, and brown-eyed. Harold stiffened when he saw him, and an annoyed look danced across his face, but he politely greeted the red-haired man anyway.

Then, the worst thing in the world happened. Miss Hypo saw me and my friends, rolled her eyes, put on a barf-inducing fake smile, and led her friend toward us. "Thomas, see how lucky we are? Here are four of my students, all quite brilliant in their own way, though I suspect they know better than to make themselves the center of attention this evening. You will all be sure to do as you are told."

"Crissy," Astrid interrupted, "I believe your assigned classroom resides outside of Braggart Estates, and as such, the only person's behavior over which you have jurisdiction or concern is your own. I trust you also know better than to make yourself the center of attention."

"And who might you be?" the red-haired man asked, addressing Astrid.

"She is a longtime associate of mine, and..."

"Crissy, please, I can speak for myself. My name is Astrid Beeswax," she said while keeping her hands clasped together behind her back.

"Hiya, fella! I'm Nova. What's your name?" I had to interrupt before Miss Hypo could.

"How nice to meet you, fellow red-headed lass," he said with a bow. "My name is Thomas Fluttergut, purveyor of mushrooms."

He gave me the creeps as soon as he called me a lass, and I couldn't talk! You know when someone gives you the creeps because they make your skin crawly. Astrid told me that if someone gives me the creeps, I should never, ever, ever stay around to find out why.

Harold must have noticed my crawly skin because he stepped in front of me and said, "Children, why don't you see how well the new supplies work right after the food is brought out?"

We ran toward the stairs before Jasper exclaimed, "YES! I've always wanted to cover someone in silly string!" He was grabbing the cans he had already stuffed in his pockets.

"I'll dump the glitter so no one else gets their hands dirty," I volunteered.

"We'll run around with streamers!" Mary Beth added, and Leo nodded in agreement. I'm happy to report that we barely restrained ourselves as we waited, twitching restlessly as we tried unsuccessfully not to giggle. But when the moment arrived, we unleashed a craft hurricane, unlike anything that anyone in Doily Dayle had ever seen!

Jasper went full bird mode, flapping and screeching like a deranged peregrine falcon as he sprayed silly string in every direction. I stood on the second floor and dumped an entire bucket of glittering doom on the unsuspecting guests. Mary Beth performed a lyrical dance with the streamers, leaving crepe paper tangled around ankles and dragged through gravy boats. Thomas the Creep screamed, "IT'S IN MY EYES!" and fell over like a fainting goat.

Miss Hypo held his head, yelling, "You nincompoops! He's deathly terrified of glitter!"

Marge and Madge turned their breadsticks into swords and bonked Miss Hypo on the head. Miss Hypo dropped Thomas's head on the hard ground, grabbed the bowl of punch, and threw it at Marge and Madge. But the punch landed on a crinkly old lady with the same complexion as concrete.

While dabbing the lady's gray hair with a napkin, Miss Hypo kept repeating, "I am so sorry, Ophelia. So, so sorry. Here, let me help you with that."

In the meantime, Leo went rogue and grabbed a tray of hot dogs. He sprinted through the ballroom as Thomas Fluttergut's five stinky dogs gave chase.

Oswald grabbed a can of silly string and turned it on Mr. Pip, "How do you like them apples, Pippy Pants?!" Mr. Pip kept combing his mustache.

When Oswald tried to stand up, he couldn't, "Darn you, Pippy Pants! What have you done?"

"Dental cement, my good fellow. Dental cement."

Chronicle the Ninth

Hiya, Everyone! It's me, Nova! Guess what? Do you want to know something? My favorite spring flower is the hyacinth, especially the blue-colored ones. Astrid says my favorite, favoritist colored ones are indigo, not blue. Either way, they also come in purple, pink, and white. Astrid covers The Bee's Knees in them and says they do a magnificent job of masking the pungent smell of unwashed humans. Yuck!

She plants the bulbs in the fall because they won't bloom before suffering through a cold winter. Astrid says people often follow the same pattern, but I don't know if she is correct because there are places in this world that receive hardly any rain, ice, or snow!

For example, the Atacama Desert in Chile, the world's driest place, remains inhabited. Inhabited means that people live there, and I bet they bloom in their own way. Not everything was meant to grow like everything else. I've heard adults say things about me like, "That wild girl will get there in her own way." Then they shake their head, raise their eyebrows, or smirk.

Smirking at someone is an act of rudeness because it makes people second-guess their great ideas! First of all, when adults say 'own way,' they usually mean unconventional or unexpected in a bothersome way. And why a child blazing a new trail and seeking new adventures in innovative ways is a bother, I have no idea.

Sometimes, Astrid uses her annoyed voice and says, mostly to herself, "We want innovation, but only within a strict set of parameters that are treated as law when they are hardly so. If everyone did what everyone else told them was reasonable to do, we would still be living outside without latrines! Surgeries would be limited to the tools used during the American Civil War, such as bone saws, chisels, mallets, and irrigation syringes. Changes are intended to improve the human condition, so why resist the curious and different among us because they challenge our current understanding?"

I recently rehearsed Astrid's point to Miss Hypo, who said I didn't understand The Cause. She also said I wasn't supposed to be hiding behind the library door, listening to private conversations. But, just like a hiding place isn't a good hiding place if people know about it, a private conversation isn't very private when held in a public space. Makes sense, right?

Also, I was hiding behind the door because I was waiting to sneak up and startle Jude the Dude after he made fun of Jasper's singing voice before Miss Hypo started talking in the hallway. She wasn't even whispering! She said I wasn't smart enough to waste her breath trying to explain The Cause. So, I told her that she might one day discover herself to be wrong and foolish.

As you can guess, I was sent to the office again. Astrid was called, and I was forced to sit in the Shame Chair and swing my legs back and forth out of utter boredom. Astrid stormed in, hoppin' mad! I wisely kept my mouth shut as the lady at the front desk scooted her chair backward a few inches. "Hello, Miss Beeswax. Thank you for coming down to pick up..."

"Hello, Greta. Before you thank me, I must inform you that I will not be removing Nova from school early because she had the audacity to ask for further explanation regarding an obvious organized effort to alter the education system, at the very least, and the community by extension. Believe me, I know. I hear many a whispering in my line of work. Knowing you not to be the responsible party for the unfolding of said circumstance, I would like to request an immediate conversation with our new benevolent and open-minded principal, as I have been informed, Horatio Beadle."

"I am he!" said Mr. Beadle, bursting out of his office with wide-open arms, as if about to hug the next person who walked by. He had teeth that were a little too big for his mouth, eyes that were a little too close together, and ears that were a little too big, plus his eyes seemed insincere.

Insincere means artificial.

I disliked him immediately, and I think Astrid did, too. He wore a waist-length cape made of black velvet on the outside and copper snake-patterned on the inside, with two snake rings on each hand: one ring was a viper eating a ruby, and three rings were king cobras choking on diamonds. (Technically, they were swallowing diamonds, but choking seems more realistic.) I couldn't wait to tell Leo about the inaccurate representations of one of his favorite animals!

"Hello, Mr. Beadle. I am Astrid Beeswax, part-time guardian of Nova Flaherty, the bright young girl you see sitting there," she gestured toward me.

"Astrid Beeswax, what an easy name to remember when coupled with such a striking woman," he said as he took her hand.

"Yes, well, I did not come here to discuss my name or appearance. I believe we have a mutual concern to be addressed posthaste! Nova has been the target of Miss Hypo's wrath for some time now, and quite frankly, it must desist, or I shall throw myself into such a fit of temper as to render us all useless. Quality education is of the utmost importance, and personal vendettas must not be permitted to become part of the course curriculum. Therefore, I humbly request a meeting with you, Miss Hypo, Nova's guardian, Mr. Pip, and a lawyer furnished by Harold Braggart. What time are you available? And, before you suggest I talk with your secretary, I trust you have a phone that tracks your schedule seamlessly and can do so yourself. I will not be put off, you understand?"

Mr. Beadle crinkled his forehead, "Braggart? Harold Braggart? Yes, yes. I do believe I have been well-acquainted with his mother in years past. I shall be delighted to meet with him."

"Mr. Beadle, you are not meeting with Harold Braggart, but a lawyer provided by him will be present at our meeting," Astrid clarified.

"Yes, Harold Braggart, let's see," he said, scrolling through his phone. "I believe I can meet with him in two days' time at three o'clock."

"Mr. Beadle, Harold will be unable to attend. I look forward to our collaborative problem-solving, and I recommend that the school board consider providing a lawyer as well. In the meantime, please allow Nova to return to class. You wouldn't want your school to earn a reputation for silencing bright and promising students, would you?" Mr. Beadle turned pink.

"To think of such an offense brings waves of nausea. We would never do that, never. I will escort her down myself and have a brief chat with Miss Hypo."

I muttered under my breath, "I'm not going anywhere with him!"

Astrid must have read my thoughts because as soon as I looked up, she winked, then turned to Mr. Beadle and said, "I'd like to see Nova welcomed back to the classroom with my own eyes. We will follow your magnanimous lead."

"Magnanimous – ah, I am that, certainly. Generous and forgiving. I do such wonderful things for children, and only wonderful people do wonderful things," Mr. Beadle said.

"So, we've been led to believe. Shall we?" Astrid sighed, waving her arm toward the doorway.

When we arrived outside my classroom, Astrid had Mr. Beadle walk in first, which was brilliant because if Miss Hypo had seen me walk in first, she might have screamed her marbles out!

Instead, she gushed, "Why, hello, Mr. Beadle. How nice of you to
visit our classroom. I was just about to tell the children how
excited I was to meet you, and now that you're here, my
excitement has been validated. Serendipitous, I'm sure. Perhaps
you could tell us a little about yourself?"

Astrid whispered, "Fortunate, not serendipitous." I'll need to ask
what those words mean later.

"Ophelia. I am so glad to visit your classroom and clear up a bit
of a misunderstanding between this, uh, this little red-haired
girl and yourself," Mr. Beadle said, trying to move his snake cape
out of the way as he turned to look at me.

"I'm Crissy Hypo, sir, and what red-headed girl might you be
referring to?" Miss Hypo asked with another smirk.

"Nova! Nova Jane Flaherty!" I declared, stepping out from
behind him with the fury of a murder of crows. When you
declare something, it means it's super duper a million times
more important than if you simply say it. Mr. Pip told me so.

Astrid rubbed her ears and closed her eyes for a few seconds.
"Pretended ignorance of your student's identity is neither clever
nor funny, Miss Hypo."

Miss Hypo didn't respond, but she flipped her blonde hair
behind her shoulder and raised her nose as if she were Goliath
mocking David. If you don't know the story, David kills the giant
Goliath with a sling and a rock.

I could tell Mr. Beadle was trying to avoid offending either
woman by pasting a ridiculous grin on his face and patting both
on the shoulder, "I do love spirited women! And bright children!
So, Ophelia – ah – I mean Crissy, you need to keep your
students in your classroom. During our previous meetings – ah
– yes, no, not our previous meetings. I must be thinking of
someone else. However, during our – ah – preparatory
schooling as educators, we are taught to encourage, not
extinguish, curiosity, and then guide the questions along until

an answer can be found through the scientific process. Right? At least I think I am right."

"Uncle Horatio! Hi Uncle Horatio! What are you doing at my school?" Mary Beth waved her arms over her head from the back row.

"Is that my dear Mary Beth? Come now, give your Uncle Horatio a hug, will you? I'm your new principal!" Mary Beth performed graceful ballet leaps until she reached Mr. Beadle's feet and threw her arms around him!

Miss Hypo rolled her eyes, "Are you kidding me? This day could not get any worse. So much for The Cause. Love and affection will be its ruin."

Mr. Beadle swung his cape over his shoulder and said, "I never pretend relations in jest, Ophelia. I mean Miss Hypo. Mary Beth is indeed my niece and the only daughter of my favorite sister. They look nigh identical, and now that I have discovered that you are her teacher, I anticipate only – ah – pleasant and hopeful reports of her experiences, which I will accept from her, not you."

"Uncle Horatio,' Mary Beth began with eyes full of adoration, 'I love you! Nova is one of my best friends! You'll soon love her as much as I do. She doesn't deserve to be sent to the office."

"Yes, I'm sure I will," he said before patting me on the head as if I were a puppy.

"Miss Beeswax, please give me the honor of taking my arm as we return from whence we came, and we can discuss items for our meeting with Harold Braggart."

"Most gladly," Astrid agreed. "Good day, Miss Hypo. Nova, I'll see you and your friends after school."

Me and Mary Beth returned to our seats and silently counted the minutes until the final bell rang. Miss Hypo said she had a headache and turned on a nature documentary about badgers.

Did you know that badgers sometimes team up with coyotes to hunt? Did you know they can tunnel into the ground and disappear from view in under a minute? Did you know that being called a badger could be a compliment since, in folklore, they symbolize determination and courage? Plus, they are resistant to snake venom. Leo is hesitant to believe the last fact.

After school got out and as we were walking to Astrid and her car, Jasper asked Mary Beth, "Why is your uncle's last name Beetle? Does he like bugs?"

She laughed, "His last name is Beadle, with a D, not 'beetle,' like a bug. I didn't know he was moving to Doily Dayle so soon. He had talked about moving when he came to visit a few months ago, but he was busy managing a charity where we used to live."

"I don't like him," Leo declared.

"Why not? He is a very good uncle," Mary Beth asked, looking sad and hurt. I decided then and there not to tell Mary Beth that I didn't like him, either.

"He thinks snakes are symbols, and when people use snakes as symbols, it usually means something bad. If he loved snakes, he wouldn't be so disrespectful to them," Leo explained.

"Oh," Mary Beth whispered, pressing the middle of her chin with her pointer finger. "There is a story about a wizard boy who liked snakes and spoke to them, and he was good."

"Yes, but he had the decency not to wear snake rings and a cape!" Jasper pointed out while Leo nodded in agreement. I didn't know what to do because I didn't want any of my friends to have their feelings hurt more and more. But I soon saw Astrid waving at us, which relieved me because she almost always knows what to do in troublesome situations.

This time, she made sure me and my friends avoided an argument by handing each of us a brown paper bag full of popcorn and a lollipop. Talking is hard to do while enjoying a lollipop. After dropping my friends off at their homes, me and Astrid drove to The Bee's Knees, where Mr. Pip and Oswald were sharing a sandwich and chuckling at jokes that were not funny. Astrid had to run an errand, so I was forced to wait for her return.

She seemed distracted and didn't smile so much, and she kept taking big sighs, rubbing her neck, and checking her watch as if she was waiting for someone to jump out at her. For the first time since we met, her smile did not reach her eyes! I was about to share my observation with her, but she was out the door and gone in two shakes!

Obviously, there was nothing left for me to do but complain! "Mr. Pip! I am bored, bored, bored! There is nothing to do here, except color pictures, paint pictures, make birdhouses, use glue, felt, and pompoms for craft projects, drink hot chocolate and eat treats, read books, practice my handwriting, write a letter, smell the flowers, sweep the floors for Astrid, breathe on the window and then spell my name in the fog, and get lost in my imagination. I trust you can see the problem I am having, as it is of the most serious and urgent nature. I am bored, bored, bored, I say!"

Mr. Pip folded his periodical and fished his toy pony comb out of his shirt pocket, "Oh, dear. I believe you have contracted a most vexing case of the 'I'm Boreds.' Unlike most ailments, the only person with antidotes is the sufferer themselves. Therefore, take a thorough examination of your symptoms and consider possible solutions to alleviate the underlying cause."

I pulled my hair up on both sides of my head and declared, "A memory just fell back into my brain! Astrid had me write a list of my great ideas a long, long, long time ago, and they've just been sitting in a collection of creative energy so full that if nothing happens, they will explode everywhere! I've learned the lesson myself: unused creative energy leads to fussiness."

"Smart girl," Oswald said, pointing his half-eaten half a sandwich at me. "When I was a boy and wanted to whittle tiny toys instead of joining the football team or other such nonsense that people tell themselves is a necessary part of boyhood, I was teased relentlessly. I tried playing badminton once, but I was more interested in the engineering of the equipment than in the game itself. I was completely frustrated until I embraced my love of toy making."

"Does Astrid have any good boxes lying around?" I interrupted. I didn't mean to interrupt, but I was forced to do so because he was talking way, way too much.

Oswald chuckled, "Astrid does not leave things, as you say, lying around. However, she may have some flattened cardboard boxes in the back."

"Yay! She says I am allowed to retrieve supplies from the back, but under no circumstances am I to work on my art projects back there ever again. Do you want to know why? Well, one time, I was wondering what her sanctuary (did you know she calls the back of The Bee's Knees her sanctuary?) would look like from the height of a giraffe. So, I wore my yellow sweats and stapled brown spots made from construction paper all over them, and I painted my nose brown with some acrylic paint I accidentally found in her secret paint stash. Then, I used all my strength to open the ladder that she had told me never to touch because she didn't want me to get hurt. But I could tell she didn't know how strong I was when she said it, so I didn't take her seriously. And anyway, just as I was taking copious notes on a giraffe's view from the top of the ladder, she walked in and gasped so loud it made me scream. Since no one can tell me definitively what sound a giraffe makes, I think they sound like a seven-year-old girl screaming as she falls off a ladder and sees her short life flash before her eyes, with her untold possibilities falling into the grave with her...Astrid told me not to say things like that because it's morbid." When I finally took a breath, Mr. Pip sat there combing his bushy white mustache, and Oswald blinked slowly through his thick, round spectacles.

Then, Astrid and her brother, Roland, walked through the door just as she finished saying, "I'm immediately suspicious of anyone who adorns their person or their clothing with snakes."

Roland put his arm around her shoulder and asked, "At the risk of your wrath, might I suggest you are in danger of jumping to conclusions and being unduly stressed?"

"You may," Astrid replied with a half-smile, "as long as I can remind you of possible unfortunate outcomes had I heeded a similar thought in relation to suspicious individuals in recent years."

I don't like it when people who love each other sound annoyed with each other, so I went to Astrid's sanctuary and promptly began an art project, using a cardboard box to make myself a spaceship on wheels. To get the wheels, I needed to borrow them from her beach cruiser bike, which she parks in front of the flower shop with decorative floral baskets. To reach the beach cruiser bike, I had to walk past Astrid and Roland while holding a hammer and a crowbar in my hands.

"Nova! Whatever are you doing with those tools?" Astrid asked, shocked.

"I need the wheels from your bike to build my spaceship on wheels," I explained.

"Are you working on projects in my sanctuary again? I thought we discussed this," she said with tired eyes.

I felt a little sad because she also looked disappointed in me, but Roland caught on to my scheme and gave me a wink. He said, "When one's mind is bursting with ideas, one can easily forget new rules. Don't be too hard on her."

Oswald and Mr. Pip caught on, too, and offered to move my project to Oswald's Tiny Toys. Then, Roland said that his wife, Lottie, would watch the shop for Astrid while he took her out to dinner. And I apologized for not asking her to borrow the bike wheels.

Astrid threw her hands in the air, gave us hugs, and drove off to spend time with her brother, whom she loves with all her heart.

I went home with Mr. Pip, and he made us some Zuppa Toscana soup for dinner while I made milkshakes for dessert. I basically had a super duper a million times good day because Astrid helped me, and I helped her!

Chronicle the Tenth

Hiya, Everyone! It's me, Nova! Guess what? I've been wearing an eyepatch for three weeks because I scratched my eye while playing Treasure Hunt with my friends. Me and Jasper were about to seize the gold and jewels from Mary Beth and Leo, when his sword got caught in my hair, causing a big fleck of bark-a-mulch to fall into my eye! I read somewhere that if you fill your hair with bark-a-mulch, you can grow a tree out of your head. But I have a few questions regarding the probability of such a claim. For example, does the tree root itself into your brain through your ear canals? Or does it slowly weave into the bone matrix of your skull and attach itself to the reptilian part of your brain?

The reptilian part of your brain, also known as the basal ganglia, bosses you around to keep you alive, basically, which means it could boss the tree around, too. Of course, I would need to choose a lovely tree to grow out of my head, not a sad or angry tree. I've given the idea considerable thought, and I would probably choose a crabapple tree because they have pretty pink flowers that change into crabapples, which means I could grow my own snacks on my head.

When I asked Astrid what she would choose, she said a lilac tree because the colors are heavenly, and the scent is even better. She had a good point, but I cannot think of a quality any tree could have better than providing snacks.

Unfortunately, because of Astrid, I'll never know the magic of head-grown trees, because she told me to wash my hair after I got wood slivers all over the back seat of her car. I could have gotten them all over the back seat of Mr. Pip's car instead, but she insisted she be the one to drive me to Urgent Care after I hurt my eye. Then, she said that washing my hair twice a week would be a better alternative to once every other week. I told her that Mr. Pip didn't care about what was in my hair or how often I washed it, and she said Mr. Pip didn't pay attention. The two concepts are not interchangeable.

Interchangeable means replacing one idea with another while maintaining the same meaning, just like a synonym! Interchangeable is a synonym for synonym. I told my friends that posthaste! Posthaste means with great speed. I think it's a British word because Charles Dickens uses it a lot in his books, and he was British. Makes sense, right?

Leo was sick this week, and he almost never gets sick, so we knew it was super duper a million times serious. We decided to visit him in his infirmity after Mr. Pip called Leo's mom and asked if we could come over. She said we could because he was recovering from a bout of food poisoning rather than carrying a contagious disease.

I expected the inside of Leo's house to have beige walls with framed sharks, snakes, and dinosaurs on the wall, but I was very wrong! When his mom opened the door, we entered a wide entryway with a stargazer built into the roof. In the future, perhaps during the winter when the night starts in the afternoon, we can have a popcorn party and look at the constellations. Leo's mom looked like a fairly reasonable woman who would be open to letting kids have fun. Plus, she had a bouquet of flowers from The Bee's Knees sitting in a round glass vase on a rectangular shelf, which shows she appreciates nature's beauty.

She guided us into the living room, where Leo was lying on a peacock-colored couch with brightly colored, velvet-covered pillows of red, yellow, green, and blue. Most of Leo was snuggled under a soft blanket covered in happy jumping frogs, but his hair, nose, and eyes were visible. His mom leaned over him, kissed his forehead, gently stroked his hair, and whispered, "Leo, open your eyes. Your friends are here to see you."

"If they want to see me, they can already," he said, his eyes crinkling around the edges and giving away his happiness.

"Very well. Your friends are here to talk with you, look at you, listen to you, breathe, possibly eat snacks, and blink. Does that cover everything?" she asked with the same crinkling eyes.

"No. Jasper isn't a boy. He is a bird. He could be a chicken, or a cardinal, or a peregrine falcon, and since birds don't talk, you forgot to list each of their sounds," Leo said, and his crinkly eyes got even crinklier.

His mom laughed and patted him on the head. "What I think I heard you say is that you love your mother very much and would like to thank her for the soft pretzels you asked her to make in case your friends come over, because soft pretzels are one of Jasper's favorite foods."

At the sound of his name, Jasper immediately dumped out his backpack full of stuffed birds and made at least fourteen different bird sounds within the same minute. He is super duper a million times good at imitating bird sounds.

All the favorites came: Sharp Beak, Blue Wing, Momma Owl, Fuzzy, and their babies. Jasper says every baby needs a mama. Yet, for some reason, he immediately sat on the rug and commenced a severe war full of destruction and death at the loudest possible pitch. Astrid calls this phenomenon a one-boy act of every war in history.

The ducks and the cardinals were hurling each other across the room with an explosion going off every time one hit the floor. Spittle and drool were flowing from Jasper's mouth, but he didn't care, and Leo laughed. Mary Beth was worried that Leo's mom would be upset by the noise, but she only brought out the soft pretzels and asked which side Leo wanted to win.

"Sharp Beak will win," he said. Mary Beth started to say something, but Jasper's war cries made a traffic jam for all other sounds. Sure enough, Leo was right. As Jasper applied his ability to multiply each bird by a thousand, a flurry of wings and battle cries filled the room until Jasper, breathless, held up Sharp Beak and proclaimed the cardinal the winner before falling on his back in exhaustion.

Thankfully, Jasper recovered quickly and somehow managed to crawl onto the couch beside Leo's feet and hug his legs. I have not any idea how Jasper gets away with hugging Leo when Leo has a strict No Hug policy. Maybe his soft heart knows that Jasper needs hugs as much as he doesn't want hugs, and Jasper's needs were bigger than his that day.

Here is a fact about Leo: once a person has a place in his heart, he'll keep them there forever.

"Would you like to hear what we learned about in class, Leo?" Mary Beth asked gently and calmly since Jasper was finally quiet. For her, she shows Leo kindness by sharing interesting facts rather than asking him questions he doesn't think need to be asked.

"Yes."

"We learned about Scottish Fold cats because Miss Hypo thinks they are cute. They are called Scottish Folds because the cartilage in their ears folds forward. They have round faces that sort of look like a smushy, fluffy owl hybrid, and they are supposed to be affectionate, curious, and soft. I've asked my father if I might have one for my birthday."

"If Miss Hypo loves Scottish Fold cats, she still has love in her heart, that means," Leo said.

"Did they originate in Scotland?"

"Yes, they did, in the Tayside region," Mary Beth answered.

"Adders are the only snake in Scotland, and they are venomous but shy. Stegosaurus footprints have been found on the Isle of Skye," Leo stated.

"I read that part of a skeleton was found on the Isle of Skye, too, and they named it Elgol Dinosaur," Mary Beth said.

Leo couldn't see her because he was staring at the ceiling, but I could see her smiling from ear to ear. She was very thoughtful in reading facts that I know she would not read on her own. Mary Beth likes to read fantasy books.

"I don't want to talk anymore," Leo said abruptly. He ends conversations like that sometimes, and you cannot be sad because he isn't trying to hurt your feelings. Mary Beth knows to expect Leo's abruptness, but she still blinked her eyes rapidly, trying not to cry.

"Leo!" his mother exclaimed. "When your friend takes the time to learn about your interests, you can at least say thank you before ending the conversation. Remember? We are still working on this skill."

"Sorry, Mom. I forgot," Leo said.

"You don't need to apologize to me, but you might thank Mary Beth before they leave," his mom said. Her voice sounded halfway between a laugh and a cry.

"Thank you for telling me about Scottish Fold cats and learning about dinosaur fossils, Mary Beth," Leo said, and I could tell he meant it.

Mary Beth could, too, and said, "You're welcome."

After we left, we all went our different ways. By the time I finally arrived at The Bee's Knees, I could not hold my words in for one more single second! Astrid says I become an erupting word hydrant when my thoughts stay in my head instead of coming out. If it's never happened to you, you have no idea of the torture! Torture, I say! Thankfully, Astrid doesn't mind being sprayed with words, so I trust her.

Here is some of what I said, just some. "Astrid, when I got my pirate patch, I decided that me and my friends should make a pirate code so none of us accidentally gets hurt ever again in our entire lives. But then I realized everyone gets hurt sometimes, even if the rules are followed. For example, I could get eaten by a tiger that escapes from the zoo and has a vendetta against little seven-year-old girls with curly red hair."

"Why would a tiger have a vendetta against little seven-year-old girls with curly red hair unless a girl fitting that description previously killed another tiger of the first tiger's family?" Astrid asked.

"Good question. I have no idea, but I know it's not impossible and might happen someday. Do you know what else might happen? I could go out on the ocean on a beautiful green boat, minding my own business, and fishing for a lark, when a blue whale's blowhole reverses and creates a swirling vortex that sucks me down, down, down into the Mariana Trench. No pirate code could help me then, could it? No. And another thing! I could get caught up in a tornado, fall into a volcano, or get caught in lava and be in desperate want of a lava-proof surfboard. I bet we could ask Oswald to make a lava-proof surfboard, just in case. Hey, Astrid? Can I have a cookie, please?"

"Please do. Nova, if I may put your mind at ease, we are not at risk of encountering volcanoes and the troubles they may present," Astrid said.

"But we are on tectonic plates. Have you ever been in an earthquake? Thank you for the cookie. I bet Leo would like your chocolate marshmallow cookies. Maybe we should bring him some, except we should only bring some after he fully recovers from his food poisoning," I suggested.

"How was your time at his home?" Astrid asked. She's good at asking questions when she wants more information instead of filling in the blanks with information she only thinks she knows. Mr. Pip says the chasm between what we know and what we think we know is often much wider than we care to admit.

"I had a real swell time. Leo's house is more colorful than I imagined, and I think that's because his mom is colorful. They have a peacock-colored couch! And, she has a bouquet from this very shop in her entryway. They have an entryway because they have a big house with high ceilings, and they have stargazers. Leo wasn't feeling too well, but I think Jasper cheered him up by performing reenactments of every war in history with his stuffed birds, and Mary Beth knew about a dinosaur fossil found in Scotland. I'm pretty sure Leo's mom would let us stay longer, but we were exhausting him," I said.

"I doubt if you were exhausting him as much as he was simply exhausted from being ill. Food poisoning can make one feel as if they are nigh approaching death. Do you think he will be back at school this week?"

"I don't know. I think we exhaust him even when he is feeling well. Hopefully, he will come back soon so I can tell all my friends about something even better than pirate code. I can't say anything if he is not there. It wouldn't be fair."

"Oh? What have you come up with?" Astrid asked.

"Pirate codes have the wrong motivation because they are motivated by selfishness. Each person thinks of themselves. Today, as I spent time with my friends, I realized that having true friends is better than rules about treasure, marooning, and mutiny. I'd still like to try and walk a plank, though, because I want to see if I can spin around while I am falling, catch the plank with my hands, and launch myself back into the pirate ship to defend my honor. We'll discuss the possibilities together. I am sure Oswald knows how to build a pirate plank. My friends are not motivated by selfishness, but by love. Leo puts his friend's needs above his wants, Mary Beth cares what her

friends care about because she cares about them, and Jasper
makes hard days better by making his friends laugh.”

Astrid put her shovel down and wrapped her arms around my
shoulders, “You have wonderful friends, Nova. And you are also
a wonderful friend because I have never known you to let a
friend stand alone. You’ve defended your friends many times,
even at risk of your seven-year-old peril. If you are blessed to
have true friends, people who love and want what is best for you,
you have more treasure than all the kings of the earth.”

“All the kings of the earth combined?” I asked.

“Yes, if you have true friends, you have a greater treasure than
all the kings of the earth combined.”

Chronicle the Eleventh

Hiya, Everyone! It's me, Nova! Have you ever been to the beach? Jasper hasn't been to the beach, and neither has Leo. Are you shocked? I sometimes forget that my friends never lived in the Pacific Northwest like I did for most of my life! It's hard to remember that what I've seen isn't the same as what my friends have seen.

We all saw a bunch of science relics together because we went on a field trip to the Payne Natural History Museum. I asked Miss Hypo who Payne was and what they did to get their very own museum, because I think it would be fun to own the Nova Hall of Flora, Fauna, and Fossils when I grow up. Miss Hypo told me that the Payne family is a very old family that has influenced Doily Dayle for over a hundred years, with a focus on philanthropy and education.

The Paynes are super duper a million times old if they have lived for over one hundred years! I bet their skin tears easily, and they probably wake up seven hundred times at night to use the bathroom. I thought Mr.Pip was super duper a million times old at sixty-seven, but he's a young whipper-snapper compared to them, and his skin tears easily. Plus, he's basically always in the bathroom every time I look for him.

Philanthropy is a word that means helping people or improving the world through giving. When I asked Astrid what the word meant, she told me to look it up in a paperback Dictionary, which I did. Astrid also said to me that anyone can be a philanthropist because everyone can be kind, and kindness is a special form of generosity. If you think about it, human history is quite generous because the museum was full of dinosaur fossils, gross specimens suspended in a sort of preservation liquid, taxidermized creatures of every conceivable kind, and old tools that humans used before museums were even thought of!

Conceivable means something that can be imagined or considered possible.

I think kids have a longer list of what is conceivable than adults, on average. Some adults still use their imagination with reckless abandon, like Oswald the Tiny Toy Maker. Astrid was going to help chaperone the field trip but cancelled at the last minute due to some "unforeseen unpleasantness requiring her attention." Instead, she sent Roland in her place.

He and Astrid look a lot alike because they are twins. Well, they are not identical twins, so their twinhood is not necessarily why they look similar; instead, it's the shared gene pool, which would have produced similar results had they taken individual turns growing in their mother's womb. At least that is what Astrid said. But even though they look alike, they are way, way different.

For one thing, Roland never ever corrects my English. He's a reasonably good speaker of English, but doesn't talk so much. Lottie told me that he prefers to choose his words carefully. Astrid runs around on her tiptoes, and Roland walks. Astrid talks through her thoughts, and Roland keeps his thoughts to himself. If they were large cats, Astrid would be a lioness because she is ferocious, compassionate, and highly social. I got those words from Astrid's paperback Synonym Finder.

You might not think Astrid is capable of being ferocious because she is so proper and fancy. But she is. Just imagine a lioness politely informing a zebra that she is about to eat them!

"I do beg your pardon on this lovely evening in the sub-Saharan African savanna, but I am most famished, as are my lion cubs, and so I must consume the entirety of your body without delay. I do beg you not to make a most unpleasant scene."

Roland would be a panther because he is quiet, stealthy, and powerful. He can take off at lightning speed when he plays hockey. I've seen it. Plus, I know that he knows more about what's going on around him than most people might think. Do you want to know how I know? I know because I can never shock him, no matter how hard I try!

If I were a large cat, I would be a saber-tooth tiger because I like to ambush people with shocking facts and glitter. But if I were a saber-tooth tiger, I would be extinct, so I might want to be a snow leopard instead because they are pretty, and, most importantly, still roam planet Earth. But they are also shy and solitary, which means they prefer to be alone. So, I probably wouldn't want to be a snow leopard either because I get bored, bored, bored when I don't have someone to talk with!

I think the Payne family is a bunch of goblin sharks because goblin sharks are sometimes called 'living fossils.' The other day, I told Leo, Mary Beth, and Jasper about my large cat theories and asked what animal they would be if they could be any living creature.

"I would be a Tyrannosaurus rex!" Leo exclaimed with his hand held high.

"I would be a chicken!" squeaked Jasper.

"I would be a ragdoll cat," added Mary Beth as she folded her hands on her lap.

"And I would eat the chicken and the ragdoll cat! Rawwwrrrr!!" Leo yelled before breaking into a wild chase.

We ran around my backyard screaming and screaming until the heat made us sweaty up to our eyeballs, and we collapsed in the

grass. I don't know why people cut their grass so short because long grass feels good on my feet, and it's softer to lie in.
"This seems like a good day for a spring butterfly," I said as we waited for our lungs to fill up with air.

"I brought my butterfly nets if you want to go butterfly hunting," suggested Mary Beth.

"I want to come, I want to come, I want to come!" said Jasper.

"Jasper, you are already here. I'm hunting for dinosaurs, not butterflies," Leo added.

"You don't have a net big enough to catch a dinosaur," Jasper said, laughing.

"Then I am a dinosaur, and I am going to catch you again!" Leo threatened with a smile on his face. We love it when Leo smiles because he doesn't do it very often, even though he is usually happy.

We were quiet for a minute, lost in our imaginations, when a raindrop landed on Mary Beth's forehead. Then another, and another, until the raindrops were landing all over! An afternoon thunderstorm was fast approaching, which meant Mr. Pip would be expecting us to run inside and ask for snacks. He must know a lot about the weather because his snacks are always weather-appropriate.

Spring and summer thunderstorms are not cold like they are in the fall and winter, but they are wet, and if you stay wet long enough, you usually get cold. Of course, we could not go inside until we had a proper romp around the yard.

Roland pulled into Astrid's driveway while we were pretending to be a herd of velociraptors, so we crept up to the fence and kneeled in the wet grass, waiting to scare the raindrops off him! But something wasn't right.

"Why does Roland look sad?" Mary Beth asked.

"What does sad look like?" asked Leo.

"Like that," Jasper answered, pointing at Roland. He was sitting in his truck with the door open, his forehead resting on the steering wheel, and his shoulders shaking.

"I think he's crying," said Mary Beth.

"We should leave him alone. He wouldn't want us to see him cry because he is a private person. If someone cries so hard that their shoulders shake, you know their heart has a huge hurt," I explained. "I know about huge heart hurts because I cried like that when my mama died."

"Didn't Roland's dad die a long time ago?" Mary Beth asked.

"Yes, a long time ago," said Mr. Pip out of nowhere. When did he creep up behind us? Maybe he is a panther, too. "Now, you children run inside and eat your buttered popcorn and apple juice."

"We can't just leave Roland alone! Someone must watch over him in case he needs a hug!" Mary Beth said, tears forming in her eyes. When she sees someone sad, her heart aches, and she wants to help them feel love because love heals huge heart hurts.

Mr. Pip gently ushered us toward his house. "Do not fret, my dear Mary Beth. I will watch over him. Now, run along, and perhaps there may yet be some happiness you can bring to Roland before the afternoon ends."

We obeyed Mr. Pip. Right before I closed the front door behind us, I saw Mr. Pip walk up to Roland's car door and reach out his arms. Roland saw him, wrapped him in his long, strong arms, and sobbed so hard I thought my heart might break, too.

Once I closed the door, we shuffled to the table to consume our snacks, and the happiness felt punched out of us. The pounding of the rain did not help us one bit. Right then, even talking felt like it required too much energy, and I wanted to take a nap. I even lay my head on the table.

"Why are you sad, Nova?" Leo asked. "You are putting your head against a hard surface, just like Roland did, so you must be sad."

"I am a little bit sad because I love Roland, and he is sad," I said.

"We could ask him to catch butterflies with us when the rain clears up," Jasper suggested.

"I feel loved when my mom reads to me. I like to listen while I play with my dinosaurs, and, if I am sad, I always feel better," Leo said.

"Nova,' Mary Beth began, 'maybe you could tell us a new story about Stuffydom."

"I want a story, I want a story, I want a story!" Jasper said as he flapped his chicken elbows.

"Are there any new dinosaurs in Stuffydom?" asked Leo.

Before I could answer, the front door opened, and drippy wet versions of Mr. Pip and Roland walked in. "Did I hear someone mention Stuffydom?" asked Mr. Pip.

I don't know how he could have heard what we were saying, because he's constantly asking me to repeat myself, even when I'm standing right in front of him. Roland, with sad eyes and a small smile, stood behind my aging caretaker and said, "I would love to hear about Stuffydom. My mom used to read to me before bedtime, and I could use a good story today."

Me and Mary Beth smiled big, and the happiness came back into the room because we were given a chance to help our friend. The thing about a chance that is given to you is that you must take it, or it goes away. We took ours as if we were opening our first present on Christmas morning. Before I could tell the story, I needed help moving Stuffydom from my room to the living room. Mr. Pip says that Stuffydom takes over the entire living room, but he doesn't mind because it fills him with youth and zest for life.

So, me and Leo, and Jasper, and Mary Beth prepared the scene while Roland and Mr. Pip changed into dry clothes and filled a bowl with fresh popcorn. Roland insisted on drinking hot chocolate, just like Astrid would have.

"Nova, before you begin the story, may I describe the scene?" Roland asked with a wink.

I had to do three jumping jacks and two twirls while I thought about his question, "Yes, you may, but if you leave out any important details, I will correct you."

"Wonderful, then we are agreed! Shall I begin?" he asked.

"Yes, yes, yes!" me and my friends cheered as we bounced on our knees and clapped our hands.

Roland lowered his voice and began, "Welcome to Stuffydom, where every available sheet, quilt, blanket, and tablecloth is gathered in an enormous pile in the middle of the floor. A tall laundry basket carries seven well-dressed girls, and a short laundry basket carries four babies. The stuffies, for whom the kingdom is named, have been thrown down the stairs and appear to have lost all use of brain and limb. Surely, life will pour into their cuddly and fluffy bodies as soon as the adventures begin.

Towels, cut-up pieces of ribbon, rope, plastic cups, yarn, beads, colored pencils, crayons, permanent markers that are not supposed to be in the hands of children, sequins, thread, rusty scissors, and dried-out glue containers. Scotch tape, masking tape, duct tape, electrical tape, and painter's tape are thrown into the pile, some in crumpled balls, setting the scene for what must surely be the most incredible story of all time. Or is it all a ruse put in place by a naughty bad guy who wants to put the innocent creatures in a cauldron, stir them together with a giant wooden spoon, and call the final result Halloween soup?"

"Roland! How can you say such a thing? I would never boil my children! It's time for me to take over because you are about to get the story way, way wrong."

He laughed, and even more happiness came into the room. Then, it was my turn to begin.

***

"Stuffydom is known as the City of Love, where bajillions of stuffies live. The Daughters, also known as my daughters, reside there and are renowned for their obsession with love and for threatening others into making marriage proposals. Even though my daughters are sometimes bad, they are occasionally good. As their mother, I would love to see them be mostly good, but you can't control your children. It's true!

Here's the sitch. Sitch is slang for situation. Astrid told me never to use slang because it does nothing to improve the clarity of a conversation and is the equivalent of consuming maple-flavored corn syrup when real Canadian maple syrup is available. If I said the word *sitch* in front of her, she would tell me that if I wanted to address my state of affairs, she would be happy to listen, but *sitch* is a deplorable excuse of a word. I would find it wise to remove it from my vocabulary with such speed and efficacy that the United States Air Force would stand in shock and awe.

She doesn't understand that, amongst children, *sitch* sounds more sneaky than situation, and I can't have a good story without some sneakiness. I reiterate, (reiterate means to repeat) here is the Stuffydom *sitch* as far as I know.

There is no quietness in Stuffydom. The noise levels are medium loud, loud, very loud, or extremely loud.

Changes are rapid in Stuffydom, so you have to pay attention and keep up because it never, ever slows down. However, sometimes stories reverse because too many stuffies are trying to conquer the kingdom and cause way, way too much damage and destroy Stuffydom.

Stuffydom cannot be destroyed, just like my soul.

The Daughters:

Samantha has dark brown hair with blunt-cut bangs and brown eyes. She wants to be engaged, but she is not. She has not found anyone who strikes her fancy. Since she doesn't know what her fancy is, she can't really strike it. Do you know what I mean? Samantha is the quietest of my daughters, which makes her medium loud. She became paralyzed after her left leg fell off while doing a front flip. She has a nice pink wheelchair that she hates. She just told me that she wants to marry the king, Spark.

Ashley has red hair and green eyes; sometimes, she likes me to braid her hair. She is the kingdom's psychopath and has a fondness for sushi and mayonnaise. She likes to throw it everywhere! She will probably marry Uglett, the black bear with black eyes and a black smile, later today. He is also a psychopath, but he is nice. They got engaged the moment they saw each other! She screams at the top of her lungs all day long, so you could say she is extremely loud.

Abigail has strawberry blonde hair, blue eyes, and is the fashion expert of Stuffydom. Abigail is engaged to the former king of Stuffydom, a dog named Davey. She loves braids, fine jewelry, her sisters, and flowers. Abigail has a heart-shaped birthmark on the side of her head. Abigail is medium loud.

Lucia has blonde hair, brown eyes, and was born with very tangled hair. Lucia loves to puke, and what's worse is that she eats it! She pukes on purpose and is engaged to a chicken named Gobble Gobble, and their wedding will be soon. A couple of years ago, Lucia had horrible head surgery after her head popped off. That was one of the saddest days because my daughter's head was detached from her body for at least two hours until the surgeon reattached it with a lot of hot glue. Lucia is loud.

Chrystalz is my only daughter with freckles, and she spells her name with a silent z at the end. She has short, ash-blond hair, blue eyes, and a partly cracked left eye. She wants revenge on Abigail because she is also in love with used-to-be King Davey and wants to impress him, but it's hard to impress him because he loves her sister. She likes to have small braids in her hair and is very loud.

Evelyn is a ballerina with brown eyes and brown hair. She puts far too much shampoo and conditioner in her hair and wants to marry King Spark because she loves him. I don't know anything else you need to know about her.

Pomegranate has brown eyes, short brown hair, and likes short braids, just like Chrystalz. She is in love with a bear named Michael, who sells BMW products. Pomegranate gets into fights easily if she doesn't get her way. She plays soccer and is extremely loud, just like Ashley.

The Stuffies:

Sharp Beak, the red cardinal, enjoys playing football and spying on dinosaurs. Spending time with his friends brings him happiness.

Turkey is a turkey who goes crazy around Thanksgiving because he thinks people are going to kill him and eat him for dinner. Rolling around like a ball and spending time with his friends brings him happiness, too!

Hummingbird is the smartest of all the birds, is a dinosaur expert, and loves to eat honey.

Red Wing Black Bird is a crazy bird that pretends he is a juggernaut who squishes his friends when he plays with them.

He stares at his friends when they roll around and tackles them when they stop.

Chicken has yet to say a single word. He can only walk forward and stare. One time, Blue Bunny, a bad guy, thought he was staring at him and captured him. He has not escaped yet.

Baby Chicken, also known as Brainy Bird Chicken, is embarrassingly unintelligent. He likes to ride on Chicken's back, and since Chicken has been captured, Baby Chicken punches his best friend Zombie to feel better. That's not a very nice way to deal with big feelings! He and Zombie have magnets in their brains that stick together.

Currently, the elected king is Spark, a gigantoraptor. King Spark is nice. Davey used to be the king, but then Blue Bunny, the main bad guy of Stuffydom, killed his wife, Juliette.

King Davey did not want his feelings to get in the way of his royal decision-making, so he stepped down as king. Blue Bunny is Huckle's toy that came to life. Blue Bunny wants to marry Lamby Lamb, and Don the purple koala also intends to marry Lamby Lamb. Don is also known as the Purple Sun because he shines a bright light that attracts people to him, so he can capture them.

Dangers of Stuffydom:

Infectious green love bugs that enter the host's brain through the ear canal and cause them to fall in love immediately. The boys fall in love with the first girl they see, and the girls fall in love with the first boy they see. However, the green love bug dies after one week, and the love doesn't last.

Love potions present the same dangers as infectious green love bugs, but at least you won't have a dead bug in your brain.

The babies. The babies are named Huckle, who is the only boy; he is cute with blue eyes and blonde hair. The others are Granny Baby, Ugly Baby, and Tiny Baby. Blue Bunny uses them as bots to help capture his enemies. People think they are cute and try to pick them up, but the babies attack them with diaper bombs and throw them in the Death Box.

The Current Conditions:

As of one second ago, Stuffydom was entirely overtaken by Blue Bunny because four of The Daughters wanted to marry King Davey and smooch him. Spino wanted to sit back, relax, and watch the daughters fight, so he gave Abigail a candy army that she used to throw everyone except Davey into prison.

The prison is made of lava and chewed-up bubble gum and is in the center of the Earth. Everyone escaped from prison when they fought Abigail's candy army with the help of Stuffydom's Continental Army.

Clone Davey had gone into Stuffydom's control tower and sent the army when Abigail wasn't watching. Abigail wasn't really Abigail; she was a pony in disguise!

Baby Chicken and Baby Zombie, the ones with magnets in their brains, tore the pony into shreds and threw the flakes at the residents of Stuffydom.

It's important to know that Baby Chicken likes to eat gasoline. It emerges from the other end of his body and propels him to fly as fast as a jet plane.

Then Blue Bunny came with his non-baby bots, which had giant Blue Bunny flamethrowers, and burned up Stuffydom. The residents were not there, so they didn't get burned because they were on their journey back from the center of the Earth.

Blue Bunny also lit Chrystalz on fire with a blue flame that never goes out, but doesn't kill her. She became a walking flame.

Then King Spark grabbed Blue Bunny, and they were both fossilized and sent into the dark abyss of space. The Magnet Brains also went into the dark abyss of space and are now trying to dig out King Spark and unfossilize him.

***

"Wow,' said Roland, blinking rapidly. 'I feel like my hair has been blown back by strong winds going one hundred miles an hour."

"Oh, Nova. What a lovely story!" said Mary Beth as she clapped quietly.

"Ba-Cluck! Ba-Cluck!" squawked Jasper.

"I only heard you mention one dinosaur. Are there others?" asked Leo.

"I've only given you the basic outline of one story in Stuffydom. There are super duper a million more details that exist. Or, we can add anyone and anything we want. It's art," I explained. "Astrid has arranged an all-class birthday party for next week since it's almost the last day of school, and she wants each child to know they are special and remembered. So, I was thinking, the four of us could put on a Stuffydom play!"

"Nope! I don't like to be in front of people. Or around people," Leo objected.

"I thought you might say that, so I made a plan B, plus it's my birthday that day. Astrid could record a video of us playing Stuffydom and then show the video to our class. We could wear masks made of construction paper and paper plates to disguise our identity!"

After a few rounds of objections on Leo's part, and plenty of candy and pie bribes, we all agreed to record Stuffydom: The First Adventure. I'll tell you all about the party next time!

Me and Mary Beth didn't tell the boys that Horatio Beadle, our new principal, would be there, or Yabutiah Itsasham, owner of Supplies for the End, or Miss Hypo's new redheaded friend Thomas Fluttergut. I think Drimwella Spindlewitt, owner of Not Your Grandma's Doily Yarn and Lace, might be there, too. Oh, and Oswald, since he owns Oswald's Tiny Toys.

We overheard Miss Hypo and another teacher whispering in the hallway about shop owners, community infrastructure, allocation of funds, and children who see too much. She doesn't know about Astrid, though. Astrid hears everything.

I once asked her why she listens to so many conversations if they sometimes cause her sadness. She said, "Because, Nova, nothing is more lucrative than knowing business that isn't yours."

You know how I say that you can learn anything if you ask lots of questions? Well, every rule has an exception, and Astrid is one exception. There are some parts of Astrid that she doesn't let anyone know.

Chronicle the Twelfth

Hiya Everyone! It's me, Nova! I had the best birthday of my entire life because Astrid took me and my friends to Not Your Grandma's Doily Yarn and Lace. I almost thought I was going to have the worst birthday of my entire life because our class birthday party and performance of Stuffydom was canceled.

Instead, we had an assembly in our school gymnasium. I like to call it the beigenasium because, as Astrid says, "The absence of color leaves one with nothing to feast upon, no nutrition for the eyes, no vitamins to nourish the creative soul."

Mr. Beadle, do you remember him? He is our new principal, and he named the assembly Educational Advancements and Their Practical Applications. There was a lot of loudness and brightness that gave me confusion. The same happened to my friends, especially Leo. He went home after the assembly because all the chaos made his body hurt.

Mr. Beadle showed us a pair of glasses called Truth Spectacles and said that, if the technology comes through, we would each receive a pair to show us what is Safe, what is Certain, and what is Easy. He promised us that if we wear them, we will never get hurt again and won't feel bad about ourselves when we fail, because the spectacles will ensure we only do things we will succeed at doing. Nearly everyone in the assembly cheered. But not me or my friends. And not Miss Hypo, either, which I found odd because she seems like she would like Truth Spectacles because they would make her job as a teacher easier.

The spectacles would control the children for her. Mr. Pip says every decision has unintended consequences, and maybe Miss

Hypo knows about one of those. She may be grumpy and sometimes mean, but she is smart. Astrid says that Miss Hypo operates far below her potential.

Potential means having the brains, talents, and abilities to become someone great.

Astrid came to the assembly! When I showed her the flyer, she said the title was unsettling and, "as such I shall be in attendance, taking copious notes."

Copious means lots and lots.

When Oswald and Drimwellla saw the Truth Spectacles, the smiles fell off their faces. Astrid looked as if she might throw up when one of the songs she often plays at The Bee's Knees started playing. The song was out of place if you ask me because Astrid does not listen to popular music, and up until then, all I could hear was popular music!

I tried not to ask too many questions on the way home from school, so I only asked what Astrid calls a generous handful. I heard her say those exact words when she explained how to measure chocolate.

"I could tell you were about to throw up during the assembly. Why? It's pretty evident that the spectacles are like video game controllers, so who is planning on controlling the children? Who made the spectacles? What if I don't want to wear them? What if they are programmed wrong? What are the parameters of safety?

Do the spectacles take increased capacity into account? I heard Mr. Pip ask a similar question when he was talking to his doctor, so I memorized it. Some things that used to be hard are now easy—for example, learning to write the alphabet. What if a kid in kindergarten learned how to write the alphabet, and the Truth

Spectacles never taught the poor child how to read? What a horrible thought! What if the Truth Spectacles put limitations on what humans can do? If they only tell us what is easy, how will we ever do anything complicated? I don't think technology knows how to factor in love. Do you?"

I think Astrid was overwhelmed because she kept taking deep breaths and saying, "Oh, Nova. I have many of the same questions. Yet, regardless of the answer, the situation smells of 1984, and the entire population of Doily Dayle is no more inquisitive than a fly drawn to honey. Be wary of anyone who promises everything in exchange for control over any aspect of your life. And, if they want control over your mind, as these spectacles are requesting while dispensing with the social etiquette of a thin veil, run."

"I know, Astrid. I just told you that it's pretty obvious the Truth Spectacles are like video game controllers. Since I'll be in danger of mind control, does this mean I never, ever need to go to school again?" I asked with my hands clasped in prayer.

"Let's not make any permanent plans about your schooling today. The foreshadowed days ahead are not immune to change. Perhaps we have hope yet," Astrid said.

"Astrid, you sound tired and sad. I can cheer you up! I bet you would feel so happy if we went to Not Your Grandma's Yarn and Lace to see your friend, Drimwella Spindlewitt. I bet you would feel even happier if you brought me, Jasper, Leo, and Mary Beth! We love to go to the store, plus we need new craft supplies for the summer. We are running low on the basics, popsicle sticks, pipe cleaners, glue, glitter, construction paper, tape, thread, string, and everything else, basically."

Astrid smiled, "You seem to know what I am giving you for your birthday already: a trip to your favorite craft store with your favorite friends. I've already arranged the date and time with their parents."

"This will be the best day of my liiiifee! I am super duper a million times excited. I won't need to be sad about my dying butterfly children. Astrid, do you remember the butterfly kit Mary Beth gave me for my pre-birthday? Remember how Mary Beth's parents believe in pre-birthday presents to extend the excitement of another year on God's green earth?"

"Yes, how many butterflies are left?" Astrid asked.

"Five of them have gone the way of all the earth, and I don't think I will ever recover! I tried to be such a loving butterfly mom! I love living things and I hate it when they die!" I started crying a little bit while I was talking, and Astrid told me that losing anyone we love hurts, even if we know we are going to lose them ahead of time.

Showing kindness to your crying friends means you don't tell them why they shouldn't be crying. While I was wiping my nose and tears across my arm, practically from my armpit to my fingertips, Astrid brought up a happier subject. "Perhaps we can bring your birthday biscotti in a picnic basket to share with Drimwella. She gave me her authentic Italian recipe many years ago, with the promise that I would share it with her on occasion. We'll add the makings of a charcuterie board as well, if you'd like."

"And homemade blackberry lemonade?" I asked.

"And homemade blackberry lemonade. We'll ask my mother if she can make us a batch. She is the original lemonade variation creator, you know," Astrid said.

"I did not know! I bet I can come up with some new ideas for her. Can we bring party hats and kazoos, too? I've always, always wanted a birthday party with kazoos. And maybe permanent markers? Mr. Pip says that the best way to show a friend how much you love them is to buy kazoos, whistles, and permanent markers for their unruly children. I think you should do the same for ruly children."

Astrid laughed, "I can accommodate your request with the understanding that you will return the items to me before getting in the car to go home, and I will keep them safe until they are needed again. Additionally, you must remind Jasper not to make chicken noises around Thistlewhistle, Drimwella's parrot. Last time we went, you may recall, the two of them got in a squawking fight until Thistlewhistle tore two holes in Jasper's favorite shirt and nearly started molting; she was throwing such an atrocious fit. That bird has no moral scruples to speak of."

"What are moral scruples?" I asked.

"A conscience, the part of your heart that tells you when you are doing something right or wrong," Astrid explained.

"Like the one time I kicked Jude the Dude in the shins and felt bad?" I asked.

"Yes, feeling bad about kicking Jude is an example of your conscience at work. Thistlewhistle does not feel bad about anything she does, no matter how rude. I would submit that she does rude things on purpose for her entertainment."

"Is that why she guards aisle seven? To be rude for fun?" I asked.

Astrid strummed her fingers along the steering wheel before answering. "I have an idea. When I take you to the store, you walk through aisle seven, observe its contents, and form a hypothesis about Thistlewhistle's motives. Bring a pencil and a notepad with you to take notes. Remember, a hypothesis is not a guess, but a proposed explanation based on existing evidence."

I don't think Astrid would survive without notes.

***

When the day of our visit to Not Your Grandma's Doily Yarn and Lace arrived, me and my friends were about to explode with excitement.

Drimwella doesn't open her store early because she likes to be awake at night and asleep in the morning. So, we had to wait patiently. We jumped on the trampoline, played tag, raced around in potato sacks, worked on the pit we'd been digging for the past three weeks, and drank all the chocolate milk left in Mr.

Pip's house! Practicing patience is easier when you find happy things to do while you wait.

"Come along, children, we must always be prompt," Astrid called out as she floated from her front door to the car, wicker picnic basket in hand.

"Why? No one else is prompt," Jasper said.

"We do not base our behavior on what others are or are not doing, even when the behavior is widely accepted," Astrid said. "How are my four little rays of sunshine?"

"We're super duper a million times good!" I declared as we climbed into her car, sweaty and happy.

"Nova, do you have your notepad and writing implements on hand?" Astrid asked.

"Of course!" I exclaimed.

"Very well, let us depart and see what treasure awaits us."

***

We arrived at Not Your Grandma's Doily Yarn and Lace at 11:30 am because Drimwella's sign says her hours of business are from 11:30 am to 8:30 pm. But the lights were off, and the Closed sign was hanging in the window, so I don't know who we were on time for.

Mary Beth must have thought something similar because she said, "I thought the store was supposed to open at 11:30."

Astrid chuckled, "You are correct. However, you will soon learn that Drimwella Spindlewitt views timing as a suggestion rather than an agreement. She'll be here soon."

"What are we going to do? I am bored, bored, bored!" groaned Jasper.

Mary Beth's eyes brightened with a thought. I've noticed her eyes always brighten when she has an idea. I've also noticed that she has a bajillion facial expressions and could probably invent her own face language. I have not shared my idea about making a face language yet because I need to ask Mr. Pip if I need to keep my observation to myself. He says I do not need to share everything I think, but I think I do. If a thought is not worth sharing, then it's not worth thinking, and every thought I have is interesting, which means I must share it.

Mr. Pip says my logic does not hold water, but my logic is in my head, so it can't hold water anyway. Maybe I should give him a lesson on water-holding objects. Sometimes I get swept away with distractions, so I'll return to Mary Beth's thought.

She said in her quiet, kind voice, "Leo, I saw you check out a book about parrots at the library. What did you learn?"

"I did some basic research on the Eclectus parrot since that's Thistlewhistle's species," Leo began as he pulled his notepad out of his backpack. He looked a little shy and a little excited. "I will tell you what I learned while we wait. The male and female look so different that scientists used to think they were different species! The boys are bright emerald green with orange beaks, and the girls are crimson red and royal blue or purple with black beaks.

Mrs. Spindlewitt probably chose the parrot because she loves colors. And, the Eclectus parrot can learn to speak as clearly as a human, but may refuse to talk if they get ticked, and sometimes they even start molting! They like to eat fresh fruits, vegetables, and flowers rather than seeds. Did you know that, Astrid? About the flowers?"

"Oh, yes, I know of Thistlewhistle's penchant for flowers. She has eaten thousands of dollars' worth over the years, which is why Drimwella and I have an understanding. She is not to bring that arrogant parrot into The Bee's Knees at any time, and I will bring flowers as a peace offering to extract the information I need from the rascal. Eclectus parrots are natural eavesdroppers, you know, and many women with secrets to tell and none to keep, talk in the aisles of craft stores."

"What kind of secrets?" asked Mary Beth.

"They swap the kind of secrets worth risking," Astrid replied.

"I don't understand what you are saying," Leo said with a tilt of his head.

"My dad says secrets aren't really secrets if you can't even keep them to yourself!" added Jasper. Astrid didn't have time to respond because Mrs. Spindlewitt pulled into the parking lot at 11:41 am in a super duper a million times old Volkswagen Beetle covered in chipped orange paint. Its engine sputtered, and the brakes screeched as she parked. Leo covered his ears.

You should know that Mrs. Spindlewitt is very short and very loud. She wears big purple cat-eye spectacles that get caught in her wavy, tangled light brown hair every time she tries to adjust them. Plus, she wears fabric. I used to think that maybe she wore funny dresses, but then I heard Astrid comment on a lack of structure, zippers, or tucks. Now I believe she has bolts and bolts of fabric at home that she wraps herself in, depending on her feelings of the day. One time, I think she wore an old curtain. Astrid says Mrs. Spindlewitt wears so many layers of textiles and beaded jewelry, it's a wonder she can drag Thistlewhistle from place to place since he lives in a huge, fancy birdcage held together by twine and ribbon.

"Good morning, Drimwella," Astrid said as she stepped out of the car. "You look as if you might need some help?"

"No need to shout! I can hear just fine," Drimwella declared as she rolled down her window and dropped her enormous, crocheted purse on the ground before heaving herself out of the car.

Today, Mrs. Spindlewitt's feelings must have been holiday-like because she was wrapped in tulle, chiffon, silk, and a golden sash that wrapped over her shoulders and around her arms like a Christmas gift. Some of her necklaces were made of big, smoothed stones, and others had old charms hanging from the ends. A thousand bracelets covered each wrist, and she wore a ring on each finger, mostly silver with turquoise, onyx, or topaz.

I once asked her what her rings were made of, and she told me. You can learn about anything if you ask lots of questions! I wonder if someday people will say, "Nova Jane Flaherty always says, you can learn anything if you ask lots of questions!"

Mrs. Spindlewitt's wedding ring is made from a real blue diamond and real gold! She said her husband, Eustace, made it for her with his own hands. She said in return, that she had made her enormous crocheted purse with her own hands so she could always see his face. Her purse is made of soft green wool with a large, embroidered gnome on the front, except it's not a gnome but a rendering of her husband, Eustace. The beard is so big it takes up the entire front of the purse, and when she pulls the flap back, rendered-Eustace tips his big red hat back, and a recording of his voice says, Hello, my dearest love. The beard is braided three inches past the chin, so it swings around. I wonder if she's ever whacked anyone with it on purpose. She seems like she would whack someone on purpose and call it an accident.

I've never seen Eustace, so I don't know how long his beard is, and neither has Astrid, but Drimwella says that when we see him, we'll know.

What if everything you carried was a reflection of what's in your brain? What about people who carry nothing?

Once she finally got herself and her fabric out of the car, she opened the trunk and pulled Thistlewhistle out with a lot of strongness and a lot of huffing and puffing before the cage crashed on the ground. Maybe she doesn't know that big things need big spaces.

Thistlewhistle squawked before we could see one of her red
feathers, and Jasper started scratching the ground with his feet
like a chicken. Before anyone could stop him, he yelled, "Ba-
cluck! Ba-cluck!" and within seconds, he was racing in circles
around Mrs. Spindlewitt's car.

"You little dickens! You're not a chicken!" Thistlewhistle said.

Jasper paused right in front of her cage, "Ba-cluck! Chickens
rule the world!"

"Here we go," Astrid whispered as she covered her ears.

"Serves you right, Thistlewhistle," said Mrs. Spindlewitt. "You've
spent your last thirty-six waking hours tormenting me with your
demand to have your name changed from Thistlewhistle to Your
Highness the Parrot of the Fourth Realm of the Winged and
Superior; you could eat a little humble pie."

"Ba-Cluck! Ba-Cluck! Ba-clluuuuuuuck!" Jasper carried on.

"You little dickens! You're not a chicken! You little dickens!
You're not a chicken!" Thistlewhistle began shrieking louder and
louder until Astrid told Jasper to stop harassing birds who are
limited to cages without ever having tasted the deliciousness of
freedom.

Thistlewhistle squawked, "That will cost you three dozen roses.
Glitter roses. Three dozen roses. Glitter roses." Then, she turned
her back and didn't make another sound.

Mrs. Spindlewitt let out a laugh and a sigh and dragged her
purse, parrot, and fabric toward her front door, which she
unlocked with a unique-looking key. Astrid used to have a
keyring with four similar keys. I wonder what she did with them.
They must have been important because she told me not to
touch them under any circumstances. And I didn't! But someone
did because they are gone!

"Nova, you get to go inside first," Astrid said as the door opened.
Mrs. Spindlewitt gently pushed me over the threshold, and I

nearly fell into my very own surprise birthday party! Mr. Pip was there, of course. And Oswald, Astrid's mom, Roland, Lottie, Mrs. Duncecap, Harold, and his dad, Frederick, and even Crocus, Astrid's dog!

"Surprise!" They all cheered.

There was an enormous purple and pink balloon arch along with a sign that said Happy Birthday, Nova, We Love You! Oswald brought his soft-serve ice cream machine with all sorts of delicious toppings: hot fudge, crushed peanuts, gummy bears, little chocolates with colorful hard candy shells, sprinkles, butterscotch syrup, strawberry syrup, marshmallows, and rainbow sprinkles!

Everyone gave me a big hug and told me nice things.

Mr. Pip: I love you, Nova. You can start saying my house, or our house, instead of Mr. Pip's house. You're the other half of my family!

Roland: Thank you for bringing light and curiosity into my life. Lottie: Your zest for life is contagious.

Astrid's mom, Beatrice: You are good. Be a good girl in the rain or the sunshine.

Harold: You're someone special.

Harold *might* become a patch in my patchwork family someday because he is one of Astrid's patches. *Might.*

Oswald: You are a girl after my own heart, so I knit you your very own Kelly-green cable knit sweater with big wooden buttons.

Astrid: I researched the Flaherty family crest. The motto is *Fortuna Favet Fortibus*, translated into English as *Fortune Favors the Brave*. You are brave. You, along with your friends, are the brave children who will shape our future. I'm blessed to be a part of your life.

Of course, my friends were ready to tell me nice things, too.

Jasper: We are friends, and I like you!

Mary Beth: You make me laugh, and I like that you keep little toys and art supplies in your hair.

Leo: You are fun, even if I don't know what you are talking about most of the time.

Kind friends and kind words are the best presents in the world, but I still like presents I can hold. So, for my birthday, I got a gift card to Not Your Grandma's Doily Yarn and Lace, and I nearly filled an entire cart with treasures. Of course, I let my friends pick out what they wanted, too, since we do so many things together and they share with me. Sharing brings all of us happiness. Oh, and aisle seven? I'll tell you more about my hypothesis next time!

If you are reading this page, I presumptuously assume you want
to read more of the eccentric cast of Doily Dayle. Delight in the
adventures of the Astrid Beeswax series!

Before the sunshine, there was a heavy storm. Read my memoir
to discover how Jesus Christ transformed my broken and bitter
life into one of joy and peace.

About the Author

Tessa Jensen lives in the Pacific Northwest with her husband, four children, a dog, and a cat. Their home is bursting with vivid imaginations, laughter, an occasional clash of opinions, and such a cacophony of noise that they are under investigation for noise pollution infringements.

Tessa earned a Bachelor of Science in Public Health from BYU-Idaho and has been practicing massage therapy for over a decade and distance running for over two decades. She loves Jesus, her family, friends, talking, crafting, baking, and making others laugh. She published her memoir, Liberated from Silence, in March 2022.

Sign up for Tessa's Newsletter

@

tessa-jensen.com

About the Illustrator

Lizzy D. Hill grew up on a farm in Southern Idaho, where she was free to explore the world around her and find the enchanting things in it. She enjoys fantasy books, researching fashion, exploring nature, and especially listening to music. Music sets her imagination off so much that most of her art is inspired by various songs and the stories she sees as she listens to them. To pursue these inspirations, Lizzy D. got an Associate of Fine Arts at BYU-Idaho and has been displaying her whimsical art at Science Fiction and Fantasy conventions and various stores and shops. She also had a successful Kickstarter for her coloring book Wickedly Whimsical Witches and has illustrated children's books in recent years. She is happily married to her best friend and living in Washington State with their son and noisy blue-eyed kitty.

Follow Lizzy

lizzydart.com

@lizzydhill